OMG

Layla F. Roberts

Contents

The Anthology

Throw your dreams into space like a kite, and you have no idea what it will bring back, a new life, a new friend, a new country . . . and a new idea, maybe? Or at least it did for me.

This time, I wanted to make things more challenging for them. I asked them to write a fairy tale retelling in space. Yes, you read it right, and boy! did these authors deliver!

Slumber

The starship looked like a cancer. Its form was misshapen, its surface grimed. Tubes snaked across the hull like vines, black and undulating. An ancient relic of the Earthbound's first Leap, the only craft never to reach its destination, Aurora drifted through the void on the edge of the universe like a malignant spore.

And yet, Gallant knew, hidden beneath that hideous shell was treasure beyond reckoning. At least, that was what the legends said. Since boyhood, he had heard tales of Aurora, the sleeping beauty, the lost craft. No two rumors were alike, though all agreed Aurora's fabled cargo was more precious than anything in the nine galactic realms. They also agreed that the ship was impossible to find.

Well, he'd proved them wrong.

Gallant had searched for nearly twenty years, scouring every star system for clues to Aurora's whereabouts. And now, after all that time, he'd found her.

He piloted his sleek solarskimmer alongside the ship's grotesque bulk. A scan of the exterior showed him an antiquated docking portal protruding from her right side. Carefully, he maneuvered his craft close enough to link with the portal. The skimmer shuddered as the heavy mechanism trundled into place. When the seal was secured, Gallant climbed into his shellsuit, hands shaking as he fastened the snaps.

When he was ready, Gallant took a deep breath, counted to three, and opened the hatch. The maw of Aurora's entry shaft yawned before him. He hesitated only a moment before stepping over the threshold. At the far end of the shaft stood a set of thick metal doors. They slid apart automatically as Gallant approached, allowing access to a long, dark corridor. Once he'd stepped through, they closed behind him.

Before continuing down the passage, Gallant paused to check his environment monitor. Miraculously, the air inside of the ship was breathable. He raised his visor and took a sniff. The corridor smelled damp, and slightly foul--but it was preferable to the stuffy interior of his helmet.

He waited a moment longer to gather his nerve, then started down the corridor. Pale green lights flickered to life as he passed, their uncertain glow casting a sickly hue. The inside of Aurora was no better than her exterior. Every surface was filthy, smeared with some darky, oily substance Gallant could not identify. Chunks of metal sheeting had been peeled from the walls; wires torn free and left to dangle like frayed nerves; lights shattered; doors bent and dented. Debris littered the floor like the husks of dead insects.

With each step he took, Gallant grew increasingly uneasy. Tendrils of fear crept into his thoughts, whispering urgent warnings to turn back, to leave this place while he still could. But no--he would not turn back. Not now. He'd come too far, risked too much to leave empty handed. The cargo. He had to find the cargo.

Driven on by visions of untold riches and the promise of a new life, he forged ahead. Corridor after ravaged, foul-smelling corridor greeted him. He suspected that this maze of hallways was leading him in circles, but it was impossible to tell--everything looked the same under these wavering green lights.

Just when it seemed that there would be no end to the labyrinth, Gallant turned a corner and found himself entering a wide, oblong chamber. The walls were lined with monitors, each displaying a fuzzy image of another section of the ship. A grey, down-like substance had settled onto everything like mildew.

In the center of the chamber was a chair on a raised platform. Gallant approached it cautiously, boots sinking into the soft greyness that carpeted the floor.

When he reached the chair, Gallant swept a hand across its armrest. Grey down dissolved into powder beneath his gloved palm, revealing the reflective surface of a touchscreen. A command console? There were no other control panels visible in the room. He gave the console an experimental tap, then nearly jumped back as the screen blazed to life. A voice boomed through the chamber, deep and echoing, yet unmistakably female.

HELLO?

Gallant gazed about him, but couldn't decide where the voice was coming from. It seemed almost to resonate within his very skull.

"Hello?" he called back.

WHO ARE YOU?

"My name is Gallant Vorn."

GALLANT... The voice shaped his name carefully, as if tasting it. GAAA-LLANT. WHAT A BEAUTIFUL NAME. TELL ME, ARE YOU FROM THE STARS?

"I..." He hesitated, unsure how to answer. His home was a farming colony on a faraway planet; a place of rocky landscapes and acidic skies.

Still, he liked the way her words sounded.

"Yes, I'm from the stars."

After a pause, the voice asked, HAVE YOU COME TO SAVE ME?

Gallant's eyebrows lifted. "Save you?"

YES. The voice became eager, almost breathless. I HAVE BEEN WAITING, GALLANT. I HAVE BEEN WAITING LONGER THAN YOU COULD POSSIBLY IMAGINE.

"Where are you?" he asked. "Are you on this ship?"

YES.

"Trapped?"

YES.

Gallant frowned. He hadn't come here to save anyone, except perhaps himself. The cargo was what mattered. But this woman--maybe she could lead him to it.

"Can you tell me where you are?"

A screen to his left buzzed with static. He turned to watch the image resolve into blurry security footage of a large, shadowy room filled with hulking machinery. In its center stood what looked like a table, perhaps meant for medical operations. Upon the table lay a form clothed in white. Though the image was indistinct, Gallant could discern that the figure was that of a woman.

"That's you?" he asked, studying the screen.

I HAVE LAIN HERE, GALLANT, IN THIS LONELY PLACE, FOR AN AGE, the voice said, her words heavy with sorrow. WAITING FOR SOMEONE LIKE YOU TO SAVE ME.

"An age?" Gallant peered closer at the footage. Though it was impossible to make out many details, the figure in white didn't look old.

I HAVE BEEN HERE SINCE WE LEFT OUR HOME, the voice replied. I HAVE BEEN HERE SINCE EARTH FELL INTO THE SUN.

The implications of her words struck Gallant like a blow. Earthbound. This woman was an Earthbound. And she was alive...

Gallant's mind raced along with his pulse. Was this what the legends had spoken of? Was Aurora's fabled cargo not riches at all, but this woman, somehow frozen in time?

It was said that the Earthbound of old had possessed strange and fantastic technology, now long forgotten. It wasn't impossible, or even improbable, that one of their number might have found a way to survive for centuries. And if this woman was an Earthbound, then she was indeed worth more than anything else in the known universe.

And even if she wasn't the treasure of legend, she would likely know where it was hidden.

"You have not waited in vain," Gallant said aloud, eyes fixed on the screen. "Tell me how I may reach you, and I will take you away from this place."

AHHH, GALLANT--TRULY WORTHY OF YOUR NAME.

There was a soft hiss, and he turned to see a set of doors glide open on the far side of the room. Lining the corridor beyond, soft green lights bloomed in the darkness to guide him onward.

FOLLOW THE LIGHTS, GALLANT. I AM WAITING...

"I'm coming," he said. It occurred to him that he had not asked her name. "What do I call you?" he asked, as he stepped into the dim, flickering corridor.

MY NAME IS ROSE, the voice replied, and it seemed to Gallant that, though unfamiliar to his ear, it was the loveliest name he had ever heard.

"Rose," he repeated, and smiled.

The passage was long, twisting, and as filthy as the others--but he hardly minded. He had a goal now, a purpose to his stride. Rose was waiting for him, and with her, one way or another, reward for his long toil.

The lights led him on, deeper into the ship. The ground seemed to slope downward, as if descending into the vessel's core. Every now and then, he heard a sound like the distant hum of a lullaby. It was a soothing melody, and helped to quiet his thundering heart.

Once or twice, Gallant called out for Rose, but she gave no answer. He had left her voice behind in the chamber of screens.

At long last, the snaking corridor ended in a final set of doors. These slid aside as Gallant approached, blasting him with cold, fetid air. Despite the insulated layers of his shellsuit, he shivered.COME, GALLANT. Rose's voice was a deep, resonating call from the room beyond. COME TO ME, MY PRINCE OF STARLIGHT.

Gallant crossed the threshold and entered a large chamber. It was the same room he'd seen on the blurry screen. Now that he saw it with his own eyes, it became apparent that the space was some sort of med bay. The room's former clinical whiteness was hidden beneath layers of thick, greasy sludge, but showed through here and there like exposed bone. Surgical laboratory equipment hulked against the walls like mutated beasts of metal and glass.

In the center of the floor stood an operating table, its various needle-tipped arms poised like the legs of a dead spider that had been turned on its back.

Upon the table reposed a woman. Eyes closed, lips slightly parted, she lay naked beneath a thin white sheet. Small clouds of frosted air rose from her mouth as she breathed. In the sickly green light, her flesh seemed almost to glow from within.

Gallant stepped closer, his own breath fogging in the frigid air. "Rose?"

HELP ME, GALLANT. Her voice echoed around him, low and desperate. I CAN'T WAKE UP. LOOK AT ME, GALLANT. LOOK HOW COLD, HOW ALONE I AM.

"I can see you," he whispered, drawing closer still. The eerie luminescence of her skin was mesmerizing. Soft waves of golden hair pooled about her shoulders and cascaded over the edge of the operating table. "You are beautiful, Rose."

GALLANT?

He pulled one of his gloves off and took up a lock of her hair, rubbing it between finger and thumb as he replied, "Yes?"

YOU THINK ME BEAUTIFUL?

"I think you are radiant."

There was a long pause. At last, the voice asked, WOULD YOU... KISS ME?

And it seemed to Gallant then, that her lips glistened wetly, and her figure was soft and full beneath the sheet, and the green light was not sickly at all but verdant and alive...

He bent forward, ignoring the subtle whiff of decay that greeted his nostrils as his face came close to hers. He hovered, eyes fixed on her closed lids, feeling the flutter of her breath against his chin.

KISS ME, GALLANT. I HAVE WAITED SO LONG TO BE SET FREE.

Her voice swelled around him, and inside of him, and it was the loudest, softest, most melodious thing he had ever heard. It was the voice of lust and love and a past long dead. It closed gentle hands around his heart and squeezed.

Gallant leaned down and pressed his lips over hers. At first, she was inert beneath him, lifeless and cold as a statue. Then, there was a twitch of movement, a soft hiss of breath, and something warm and wet slithered into his mouth.

The slick, sinuous thing slid across Gallant's tongue and down his throat as quick as thought. He reeled backward, choking and gasping as the warm wetness filled his gullet and surged down into his belly.

On the table before him, the woman was changing. A long, wheezing gasp escaped her lips as they peeled back into a hideous rictus. Her body convulsed, tensed, began to curl in on itself. In moments, the supple young form was replaced by a contorted frame of skin and bones.

Gallant coughed violently, staggering as he backed away from the grotesque spectacle. Fluid spilled from his mouth, bitter, dark and sticky. Something moved inside of him; a writhing, slippery mass. He turned toward the doors by which he had entered, but found them sealed. Without trying, he already knew they would not open for him again.

Struggling for air, Gallant fell to his knees. His eyesight dimmed as the roiling in his guts increased. It was as if he'd swallowed a bucket of live eelworms that were now frantically trying to escape.

GALLANT?

The voice had changed too. It no longer sounded female, or even human.

BEFORE YOU SLEEP, GALLANT MY LOVE, I WANT TO THANK YOU.

Gallant shuddered as something soft and fragile inside of him burst. The dark fluid was pouring from his lips now, a steady, cloying stream that pooled about his knees. He could no longer speak, or breathe, or think...

I WAITED SO LONG, YOU SEE. THIS SHIP, THIS ENDLESS, CURSED DARKNESS... I HAVE BEEN SO ALONE, TRAPPED IN A SLUMBER LIKE DEATH...

Gallant slumped forward and fell, jerking and twitching as the being inside him slithered freely among his organs. Darkness closed in, drawn like a curtain across his sight. He was cold. So cold.

The voice spoke in his mind one last time, low and sibilant:

BUT YOU, OH, YOU, MY SWEET PRINCE OF STARS... YOU HAVE SET ME FREE.

Breadcrumbs

"We're lost."

"We're not lost, Greta." Henry tapped the fuel gauge and watched the dial spin in a furious circle. He tapped it again, harder and frowned.

"We're lost and we need fuel. Great." I slumped in my seat and stared through the glass shield at the endless black expanse.

"Another hour and we'll be space debris."Henry made a face, scrunching his narrow nose. "Stealing dad's ship was your idea. He won't come after us, you said. He doesn't care about anything except his bottle of gin, too drunk to notice the ship is missing. And you were right. He doesn't care about anything, especially keeping the ship's tank full." Henry cast the fuel gauge another disgusted look, and then climbed out of his seat. He paced the deck, fists clenched.

My brother was worried. Nothing new. He worried about everything, but most of all, he worried about me. About the way our father got angry, so angry, he punched the walls. Broke things. He worried he wouldn't be there when dad stopped using inanimate objects to vent his rage and started using me. Henry was older by three years, and since he'd just turned eighteen, he'd be forced to join the galactic fleet and serve his time. That left me alone and three years short of joining the fleet myself. A lot can happen in three years. Bad things.

"I didn't have time to check the gauge before we left. You climbed aboard and told me to punch it, so I did. We'd still be on Garvine if I hadn't gotten us out of there. You weren't in any condition to fly." I braved a glance at his left eye, the tissue beneath swollen, skin turning a dark blue. The injury should have been mine. We weren't twins but I felt that phantom pain as if we were connected on a deeper level. Maybe we were. Henry had stepped in front of me. He shoved me aside and told me to run. The plans we'd made in secret, plans we never really had the courage to act on, suddenly became reality.

We ran, stole dad's ship, and entered free space. Henry was now a fleet defector and I was a runaway. And now, we were lost.

With no fuel.

How long would we drift before we ran out of supplies? A week? Two? We could send out a frequency and try to signal another ship, but we'd already traveled so far out of the galaxy, and there hadn't been anything on the radar in hours.

I scanned the mass of star clusters, searching for anything that might resemble a planet. Nothing, just hot gas and their pin pricks of light. A well of guilt overflowed in my stomach. If we died out here, it would be my fault.

"I'm sorry, Henry." My voice felt thick with unshed tears. A painful lump made it difficult to swallow, and my vision blurred, the stars becoming streaks of white light.

"Don't say that." Henry wrinkled his brow and sighed. He looked older than his years, features ragged with the truth of our situation and the responsibility of keeping me alive. It wasn't supposed to be his job, that's what parents are for. But, we'd been dealt a poor hand, a mother who left when we were young and a father who never got past it.

The red fuel light flicked on, and I bit down hard on my lip to stem the sob in the back of my throat.

"Warning. Warning. Low Fuel." The electronic voice sounded sad to my ears, and I almost laughed to think a disembodied voice felt any sympathy for us. So long electronic lady, we had sealed her fate too.I blinked back the tears and swatted at one that tried to escape. Henry still paced, his steps growing more forceful with each second.

Ding!

The tinkling bell of an incoming message lit up the screen. I stared in confusion at the flashing message, then swiped the glass and tapped the open button. Henry moved behind me, leaning over my shoulder. We read the message, then looked at each other.

"It's a map to an outpost," I said, turning back to the screen.

"Breadcrumbs," Henry murmured.

"What?"

He pointed at the words above the coordinates. "Brash Rumb. It means breadcrumbs in the old language. You follow them home."

"I like the sound of that. I like the sound of anything that isn't deep space. I say we go there. We can make it on the fuel we have left. Someone sent that message. We can ask them for help."

"We don't have much choice." Henry's voice was low, troubled. I nudged his arm.

"Stop worrying so much. Everything will be fine."

***

The outpost appeared out of nowhere, a dome shaped structure floating in the inky blackness like a mirage in the desert. We docked the ship, coming in on fumes. Either we'd get refueled or this hole in the dark was our new home. I just hoped they had food and a shower.

Henry radioed our arrival, but there was no answer. He looked uneasy, leading the way off the ship.

"Hello? Anyone there?" His voice echoed down a stark white corridor. Harsh light made me squint.

"We come in peace," I said, smirking as Henry rolled his eyes. We walked down the sterile hallway to the end, stopping in front of a large metal door. Henry knocked. We waited until the eerie silence got to me and I reached up and pressed the little green button near the handle. Henry grabbed my hand, trying to stop me, but it was too late.

The door hissed open.

Soft music spilled into the corridor and the barren hallway gave way to small eatery. Red, plastic cushioned booths and laminate tables dotted the room. The floors gleamed, forming pools of light from overhead pocket bulbs. I smiled as heavenly scents assaulted my nose, fried chicken, french fries, and something sweet like apple pie or cinnamon buns. All the booths were empty, and we hesitated in the doorway.

"It's just like the old diner back on Garvine. The one we used to sneak to after Dad fell asleep on the couch." I stepped into the room, searching for the owner. It was so strange. Everything was the same, down to the jukebox in the corner. I could almost picture us huddled together in the far booth, dipping fries in a puddle of ketchup, and planning our escape.

"Greta, I'm not so sure about this place." Henry still stood in the doorway. "Let's go back to the ship."

Pots and pans clattered beyond the swinging doors, and I turned to find the doors fling open and a short, pudgy woman shuffle into the room. "Welcome to Ginger's diner. You kids look starving. Pick a booth while I get you some menus." The woman's shoes squeaked on the linoleum as she grabbed two plastic menus and followed us to the corner.

"You two are awful far out. Is it just the two of you?" She plopped the menus on the table and pulled a pad of paper from her apron.I nodded and scanned the menu. I wanted everything, but we had to be frugal. Fuel was more important than our stomachs.

"Get a burger," Henry muttered. "I'll eat some of your fries."

The waitress clucked her tongue. “Nonsense. You’ll both get burgers. It’s two for one Tuesdays here at Ginger’s.”

My stomach rumbled giving away my hunger. I glanced at the waitress’ name tag. “Thanks Luanne. We’d love that.”

“We need to refuel too.” Henry slid his menu aside and took another wary look around the diner. “Not many customers. Where is everyone?”

Luanne flashed a wide smile. “It’s the slow season. This place really gets hopping when the meteor showers come this way.

Everyone flocks to Ginger’s. We have the best view.” She picked up the menus and turned on her heel. “Two burgers with fries coming up. Do you want milkshakes with that?” Not waiting for an answer, she burst through the kitchen doors, leaving them to swing wildly in her wake.

“I don’t like this place,” Henry whispered.

“It’s weird how much this place looks like the diner back home. How is that even possible?”

I shrugged. “Does it matter? They have food. We can get our ship up and running again, and maybe Luanne can give us directions to the closest planet.”

Henry frowned and leaned back in his seat. Luanne re-entered the room, humming to the music piped in from hidden speakers. She swayed her hips, and did a little shimmy; all while holding two frothy vanilla milkshakes. Depositing the milkshakes on our table, she wiped her hands on her frilly apron, and then hovered until we took our first sips.

"Delicious," I said, licking my lips. The sweet, icy vanilla flavor coated my tongue.

"They should be. Milkshakes are one of Ginger's specialties."

"And where is Ginger?" Henry chuckled, taking a long swig of his shake.

"I ate her."

I choked and covered my mouth so I wouldn't spray vanilla all over Henry. The sugary sweet drink threatened to rise back up my throat. "You what?"

"Lord, look at your faces." Luanne cackled and swatted her thighs. "You believed me, didn't you? Such innocent children."

Henry's features paled, and I looked at him, watching as his eyelids drooped. He forced them open, and his mouth parted, but no sound came out. Something oily, like fear slid through my veins. The room tilted and swirled. My vision narrowed, and like Henry, I couldn't keep my eyes open. I heard a sharp crack, realizing too late that my head had hit the table. Henry's milkshake tipped over as he tried to reach for me, but his clumsy hands slid through the icy liquid.Luan ne leaned over us, still chuckling. She used a rag to wipe up the shake before it spilled onto the floor. I struggled to remain conscious, and as my eyes closed for the final time, her voice sounded near my ear. "I didn't eat Ginger. But, I'm going to eat you."

***

I woke up with a gasp. It was so hot. Sweat drenched my shirt, making the fabric cling to my skin. I moaned and rolled onto my side, still fuzzy from the effects of the drugs.

"Shhh." Henry crawled to me and pressed a finger to his lips. He pointed up to a steam-covered window where a large silhouette hummed a fast tune on the other side.

"Where are we?" I whispered.

"Some room off the kitchen, I think."

My head pounded, and I rubbed my temples as I took in the cramped room. Boxes were scattered over the floor, shirts and shoes spilling from their insides. A pile of pants took up one corner. I silenced the cry that threatened to burst past my lips. There had been so many others. We sat in a graveyard of clothes, their owners a victim of Ginger's specialty.

"She said she was going to..." I couldn't finish the sentence.

"Not she...it. Luanne's not human."

"What are we going to do?" Hysteria tinged my voice, and my breath hitched.

"We're going to get out of here."

"How?" I looked at my brother. The one who always had a plan. Always knew what to do. Except this time, I could tell he didn't know. Which meant for the first time in our lives it was up to me. I couldn't hide behind him or let him step in front of me the way I had with our father. We'd run away because of me, and now, I had to be the one to get us out of a jam.

I scanned the room, trying to come up with a plan to kill a human-eating alien with only a pile of clothes. And there it was. Almost covered by a leather jacket was a grate in the wall.

"Help me get this open." I curled my fingers into the metal mesh, waiting for Henry to do the same. The grate came loose, revealing a narrow tunnel.

"I'll go." Henry nudged me aside.

"You won't fit. It has to be me."

He frowned, big brother disapproval plastered across his face. Beyond the window, non-human Luanne lifted a butcher knife into the air and thunked it down on an unseeable object.

"It has to be now." I gripped Henry's shoulder. A curse and a protest formed on his lips, but I ignored him and slid head first into the tunnel.

I barely fit. The passage squeezed me on all sides like a snake swallowing its prey. I slid deeper, the darkness chewing me up. A ninety-degree turn appeared, then a shimmer of light through another grate. This one took all my weight to remove, and I burst into a dimly lit room. Rows of monitors gave off an electronic glow. In one, I saw Henry, still peering into the grate after me, in another, Luanne gathering spices into her apron. A monitor showed our ship docked and the diner from every angle, except from this perspective, the diner didn't look the same. Gone were the red plastic seats, the jukebox, and classic memorabilia. Rusted, dirty tables were in their place. It was all an illusion.

My eyes flew to the controls, and there it was, a memory projector stick. The device could hack into a person's memory and show them what they wanted to see, what made them most comfortable. It had lured us in and set Luanne's trap.

I jerked the stick from the port and crushed it beneath my boot. The monitor flickered and the on the screen, Luanne turned, her eyes meeting the camera. Her friendly human waitress disguise melted, revealing shiny green scales, a thin face with round eyes that burned red. I searched the controls and found the little red button they always tell you never to push. My thumb came down on it hard. The monitors winked out, and so did the power. The room plunged into darkness, and as I crept out into the hall, I whispered, "I'm coming for you."

***

The only light came from a massive pizza oven. Heat radiated from its open mouth and the coals glowed orange. Silence as deep as space itself hung in the air. I scanned the kitchen, my eyes adjusting to the low light. Luanne was hiding. Fear climbed my back and slithered along my neck.

A cast iron pot clattered to the floor. I sucked in a breath and slipped around a metal work table. Soft laughter reached my ears.

"I was going to save you for later, but looks like I'll have to cook you first."

Heart knocking in my chest, I reached for a weapon, my fingers closing on a spatula. Not helpful. Next to it was a ceramic bowl filled with a chalky substance. Flour. An idea took shape. I picked up the bowl and edged closer to the oven. More laughter sent shivers up my spine.

"I can see you."

"Not for long," I muttered. The attack came from the left. Luanne charged, her oily scales glinting. Her butcher's knife sliced through the air. I spun and threw the bowl of flour. A million white particles coated her face and eyes. The knife clattered to the floor as she swept thick, green fingers over her face. Blinded, she stumbled closer to the oven.

I didn't see her in that moment. I saw my father's enraged face. I saw the unfairness, the childhood that had been stolen from me, and the fear that had forced my brother and I to run for our lives. We'd run from evil only to find a different kind.

The flour settled, and I lunged, pressing both hands against Luanne's back. She hit the edge of the oven, teetering into its gaping mouth. I dropped low and lifted her up, thrusting her inside. She screamed, the sound cutting off as I flipped the iron door closed.

Air rushed from my lungs and my chest heaved. I smiled, swatting flour from my hands. Fear slowly ebbed as reality sunk in. I hadn't run, instead I faced evil and won. I could do it again. Running away hadn't solved our problems, but it had given me the courage to face them head on.

I left the kitchen and unlocked the room holding Henry. He tumbled out and pulled me into a tight hug. His face went slack in awe as I told him what had happened.

"What do we do now?" He asked.

I took a calming breath. "We go home."

Puss in the Boötes

Marcus didn't like the smug look on his sister Elva's face, but he didn't ask questions. If she knew, she'd never say why Dad suddenly called a family meeting. His stomach knotted. Whatever Dad was up to couldn't be good.

They crossed space station Carrabas to the processing module and found Dad in the control room. He sat in the primary operator's chair, his hands clutching the armrests, though three missing fingers probably weakened his grip. It was hard to tell what he was thinking since radiation burns left one side of his face immobile.Their brother Zen hurried in and latched the door behind him. "Sorry I'm late, but analyses came in on another load of asteroid ore. I told that sorry excuse for a prospector to sell his rock elsewhere if he didn't like our offer."

"That's my boy. Makes me sure I'm doing the right thing." A smile lifted one corner of Dad's mouth. "I'm going home to Earth, kids, to retire on a tropical island and watch birds fly through blue skies for the rest of my life. Your step-mom's booked us passage on the Big Dipper and it leaves dock in an hour."

He waved their shocked protests into silence. "No time for good-byes. Message me if you must. I'm here to give you each your inheritance and then I've got to go.

"The refining operation belongs to Elva. I know she'll make a profit." He heaved himself out of the chair and she slithered into his place.

He tossed a memory cube to Marcus's older brother. "Zen, here are the command codes to the Sagittarius. Hauling ore is up to you now."

The next memory cube hit Marcus in the chest and fell to the floor. He was too stunned to catch it, because he knew what remained among his father's holdings.Dad looked him straight in the eye. "Marcus, the Boötes is yours. Try not to crash on your first flight, will ya?"

***

Puss crept onto the tiny bridge of the Boötes. As the only crew, little escaped her notice on the prospecting vessel, but she'd have to be deaf to miss a sobbing human sitting in the pilot's seat.

The man held a memory cube over his head. "What am I going to do?" He certainly wasn't asking Puss. He hadn't heard her arrive on soft padded feet or looked down into her double-lensed eyes.

He didn't appear to be dangerous, so she spoke to him.

"Do about what?" Her translator rendered her words as human speech.

The man jumped and wildly scanned the narrow bridge.

"Down here. I'm Puss, engineer on the Boötes."

Her appearance startled him out of his tears. "You're a billee, aren't you? I didn't know my dad hired any of your species. Did you come with the alien colony? To serve the raakshas?

Puss's short tail flicked with irritation. How could he think she was that old, when her fur was glossy black? "My parents arrived in the Jupiter system with the colony, but I prefer humans to raakshas."

The man slumped against a console but, at half his height, that still left Puss staring up at him. He sunk back into tears and, with a flick of her tail, she realized he had dismissed her as inconsequential. This was not unusual. Her snub nose and thick fur made many humans call her cute. She'd accepted the name Puss before she realized how that added to her cuteness. But humans had to take her seriously when she turned her glowing copper eyes on them. She gazed at the man that way now.

"Where's my pilot?"

"Dad fired him. This is my ship now, and here's everything else I own." He swung a yellow gym bag that flopped, half empty. "I'm broke."

Puss tilted her head. "There are fine samples of crystals in the Boötes' hold."

"A temporary reprieve. I haven't got a pilot's license, so I'll have to sell the ship as soon as I can."

A squeak escaped Puss's throat. Some humans, even here in the asteroid belt, resented aliens. They were willing to use the portals the raakshas scattered across the Sol system, but obstinately believed a billee belonged on Jupiter's moons.

Puss feared losing her home onboard the Boötes if such an individual bought the ship. She had to help this pitiful human. "There's a piloting class starting in two days, so sign up."

"Already failed the test."

"Well, lots of people have to take the test twice."

"I already failed twice."

Puss was glad her whiskers hid a frown. It wasn't smart to frown at her new boss.

"Three's the charm. Isn't that what humans say?"

"How will I pay for the class?"

"My dear boss..."

"Marcus. Call me Marcus."

"My dear Marcus, don't fret. Sell the samples in the hold and let me use your command codes for the Boötes. I will secure you a living while you study piloting."

Puss couldn't always read human feelings, but she thought Marcus looked hopeful.

"Well, why not?" he said. "I never expected to be abandoned by Dad, but 3never expected to meet a billee either." He dropped the memory cube into her thick-fingered paw.

***

Whether the Boötes was a small ship or large robot could be debated, but either way, it was a fine craft for prospecting. Early the next day, Puss undocked and headed anti-spinwise to a special asteroid she'd spotted on the scanners. There she sank grapplers into the rock and used forward manipulators to explore beneath a layer of stardust.

Yes, there it was.

She sealed the crystal in a glass autoclave jar and used aft manipulators to stow it in the cargo hold. Once the hold repressurized, she clomped down the short passageway in her magnetic boots and opened the hatch.The thick glass jar felt cold from space, even against her padded fingers. Inside was a fine osmium tetroxide crystal as big as her head, clear with a pale greenish tinge along the edges. "I've kept you a secret for a long time," she said. "But I face an emergency now. My boss could sell you and live as a wealthy man for a year on Carrabas, but then what?

"As my old Dah used to say, if nothing changes, then nothing changes. So I'll try something new and see where it leads."She skipped the Boötes through several portals dispersed within the asteroid belt to arrive at Carrabas station's great rival on the opposite side of the sun, the colony of Wángguó.

When the dock controllers demanded to know her business, Puss said, "I have a present for your Chairman. Please let me dock and pay homage to him."

She towed a wheeled bin to the Chairman's office, was escorted inside, and bowed low.

"My boss sends this crystal to Your Excellence with his respects." She lifted the glass jar and the Chairman's eyes glowed. No human would have ever seen an osmium crystal so large.

"I am obliged to your boss," he said.

A young woman approached the chairman's desk. Her eyes sparkled and her black hair hung in a sleek, glossy braid. "Dad, don't you think we should thank the billee who delivered such a fine crystal?"

Puss had heard the Chairman's daughter was his Chief Executive Office. She smiled at Puss, obviously as wise as she was beautiful, and the billee purred.

"My personal assistant will arrange quarters for you," the CEO said. "Also a full credit cube with my compliments. I'd like to meet your boss. Perhaps you'll arrange that for me?"

***

Puss ordered a meal delivered to his elegant quarters. Not the dehydrated stuff he ate aboard the Boötes, but fresh grubs, plump and alive. She spoke to them as she munched.

"I wouldn't mind making this colony my permanent port. But how am I going to turn a human who can't pass a piloting exam into a proper mining boss?"

She called up Sol system maps and studied reports of various prospecting operations. Most raakshas stayed among the moons of Jupiter, but one had a mining outpost. If it was as cruel as other raakshas Puss knew, rumors that its miners felt little loyalty would be true.

That night she visited bars where some humans were pleased to talk to the first billee they'd ever met. She discovered that the CEO enjoyed cruising through the asteroid belt in her ship, the Orion, and learned her flight plans.

Puss's research formed the basis of a plan.She left the colony dock with a full load of fuel and, in less than a day, found a mining vessel beholden to the raakshas' outpost.

The vessel dug ore autonomously so the pilot, bored, opened comms.

"Would you be willing to say that your outpost is owned by my boss, Marcus?" Puss asked.

The pilot snorted. "Happy to say it and happier if it were true."

"I'm transmitting an image of my boss. By the time you return to your home dock, it will be true."

"Then I'll owe you a favor, and I'll tell all the pilots in our fleet they owe you too."

***

The Boötes popped from the portal on a clever vector, putting Puss at the outpost's centerline. The dock controller challenged her at once.

"I heard this is an imposing outpost," Puss commed. "Run by an impressive alien, so I came to check it out. But I see nothing special."

"B... belay that." The controller stumbled over his words. "Our owner monitors this frequency and doesn't tolerate criticism.""Then it should have constructed a decent outpost."

A gravelly voice boomed through the translator. "Who dares speak with such disrespect?"

Pulse cannons pivoted and locked onto the Boötes.

Puss trembled, her pulse racing, but the translator held her voice steady.

"You have pretty guns, but they're mounted on the outpost." She swung the Boötes through a carefree figure-eight maneuver. "I doubt you can catch my ship."

A roar over comms knocked Puss back into her seat. The controller announced on all channels, "Make way for the owner's scout ship."

A raakshas ship launched from the dock and Puss spun the Boötes around. She dodged a laser blast by angling through the nearby portal.

From portal to portal, the Boötes seemed barely ahead of the raakshas but always just beyond its laser's range.

At last, Puss popped out above the paisley storms of Jupiter, emerging on a vector that skipped across the top of the atmosphere. The raakshas rocketed straight out and into dense clouds. Its scream of rage turned to terror as the scout ship plummeted, trapped by the giant planet's gravity. It was crushed into silence long before reaching Jupiter's metallic hydrogen core.

***

Puss docked the Boötes in a cheap, outer bay at Carrabas station and went to search for Marcus. She found him sleeping in a passageway.

He staggered to his knees and hugged her in a grimy embrace. "Puss. I thought you'd stolen the Boötes and left me to starve."

"Never, Marcus. How'd the piloting class go?"

His face flushed an odd pink color. "Much better, actually, than last time. I only failed the exam by one simulation."

She patted his bare, clammy hand. "I have food and clean clothes for you on the Boötes. Refresh yourself and do whatever humans do to appear attractive to each other."

At the mention of food, Marcus followed her. He ate and then slept until she woke him. They were hovering over an asteroid with a large central crater.

"Don a spacesuit," Puss said. "Go out through the cargo airlock. For heaven's sake, take a rock hook with you and don't fall off the asteroid until I return."

Marcus's eyes widened. "You're leaving me here?!"

"For less than a day. Remain calm so your air will last. Spend the hours memorizing instructions I loaded into the suit's memory." He could view her instructions dozens of times while he waited. Puss hoped even Marcus could remember after that.Marcus's mouth hung open a moment. "I never expected to be left clinging to an asteroid. But, I never expected to meet a billee either. I'd rather die than sleep in passages and eat from trash compactors again. I'll do it."

***

"Mayday, mayday, mayday." Puss sent the message as she streaked towards the CEO's ship.

"Puss?" came the reply. "What's wrong?"

"Is that the Orion? What luck to find you. My boss, Marcus of Carrabas, is adrift in a spacesuit."

"What? How'd he end up in such a state?"Puss couldn't always read human voices, but the CEO sounded disappointed.

"He enjoys cruising through the asteroid belt, but pirates seized his ship and dumped him in the airlock. He did not despair. He donned a suit before they ejected him into space."

This time, the CEO sounded bubbly. "Lead on, Puss. I must rescue such a resourceful man."

In a few portal hops, they arrived at the asteroid and the CEO took Marcus onboard.Puss opened comms. "My boss's outpost is nearby. Follow me."

The dock controller greeted Marcus by name. "Boss! It's such a relief to have you home. Bring that ship into the center bay."Puss sidled the Boötes in quickly and met Marcus and the CEO as they emerged from the dock. She led them along the main concourse and, from both sides, miners shouted Marcus's name. The CEO slipped her hand into his, stepping lightly at his side.

They climbed a platform at the end of the concourse, and Marcus addressed the crowd. "Miners. This close call with death makes me realize what's truly important in life. I hereby grant eighty percent of this outpost's shares to you, to be divided equally."

The CEO beamed at him with, Puss felt sure, deep admiration.

Cheers became deafening. The CEO shoved fingers in her ears but Marcus waved and smiled, just as Puss had instructed. She'd explained in her recording that twenty percent would make him wealthy and also free from administrative duties.

***

It didn't take long for the cheers to subside and the miners to, either, retire to bars or surround the outpost's solicitor's offic e.Puss followed Marcus and the CEO back to the dock and they left for Wángguó colony. Apparently, Marcus had done a fine job of making himself attractive, because the CEO fell in love with him. Perhaps his obvious courage and generosity were attractive too.The CEO assigned some splendid quarters to Puss, with all the grubs and other fine things she might want. Marcus never asked her to return the Boötes command codes, but from then on, she only prospected for fun.

And they all live happily ever after.

The Nightingale

In the summer of 2941, the Great Emperor of China was turning seventy years of age. His birthday would mark his Golden Reign of 50 years as our ruler.

I was barely a man at that time, a young boy hovering between the folly of youth and the responsibilities of an adult. I lived on a small island on the opposite side of the river of metropolitan China. I often wondered what the big city would be like, for I had never travelled any place further than my beautiful Tree Island. Story books I read as a child spoke of a China I never met, a place that was not dotted by tiny islands covered in flowering trees. There wasn't the abundance of rivers and lakes of now. The sky above used to stink of pollution yet now it rested peacefully in a perpetual summer's blue, lightly laced most days with a delicate mist.

My father was a farmer, my mother sewed. I was a poet. I spent most of my time on the grassy hilltops, watching the city quiver behind curtains of pale fog as wild birds serenaded me. In the evenings, I camped under the stars with my flashlight, my notebook, and my quill to write about everything my heart longed to say. My parents took pride in my written work. I won many awards with my poetry over the years. My mother said that one day I'd become a famous author, move away and forget about their humble existence.

"Never, mother," I told her. "I would never give you and father up."

"Even for the poetry you so love?" She asked with a delicate small, yet I saw tears glisten in her warm brown eyes.

I threw my arms around her and shook my head. "I love you more than the silly words I write."

"When you are famous," she said, "people will give you grander gifts than those we have been able to give you." In her wrinkled face I saw depths of love. Both mother and father raised me well. I never wanted for anything, be it food, shelter or, most importantly, love. I was their only child, a blessing, as they said, after twelve years of still-born births.

"You gave me life," I whispered, my heart swelling with the love I carried for them. "This life gave me words, joy --" I paused to look towards the caged nightingale on the kitchen table, "and song."

On the center of the table sat a humble wooden cage my father made for my birthday last year. Inside the cage was the little brown nightingale my mother caught. Every night, the bird's singing filled our small home with happiness for there is no grander melody than that of a nightingale.

Over the centuries, these little birds had grown scarce. Once found all over China and its perimeter, Tree Island was now the last area in all of Asia where these tiny creatures nested. Here they began to flourish. In the last few years their numbers doubled. Soon they would look for new homes, perhaps one day they'd make their way to other parts of Asia as they had years ago. I opened the bird's cage and held out my hand. She fluttered her wings and perched on my finger. I smiled in hope that one day her offspring would find their way to the capital where they could perch on the golden nightingale statues surrounding the Emperor's palace.

Now June rolled into July and eventually August came. During this time, I wrote a handful of works which I sent to China to be published in one of the newspapers. When my copy came, the post man also handed me an official looking letter and asked me to sign for it.

Curiously, I looked at the thick cream envelope as I scribbled my signature.

"Have you won a competition, Deshi?" The postman asked.

I shrugged. "I haven't entered one," I flipped the envelope over and looked at the sender's name in awe.

The emperor's official stamp stood out in bold type. His insignia, the Golden Nightingale, looked back at me. The bird's delicate feathers fanned across the envelope. Above, my name was neatly handwritten.

"You must have won something. That's a letter sent personally from the Grand Emperor himself. Perhaps it is an invitation to the Golden Reign."

I looked up at the postal worker . The Great Emperor would be hosting a party for his dual celebration in two weeks. He'd be choosing two citizens that had offered something of beauty though their art as his honored guests.

There was a big smile across the postal worker's face. When he saw the dumbstruck look on mine, he chuckled. "Go and read it in peace. I'm certain it's fabulous news."

Mutely, I nodded. I couldn't even mutter a thank you.

As I rushed into the kitchen, the newspaper slipped out of my hands and papers fell onto the floor. I bit my lip to keep from swearing. I always kept any newspaper or magazine I was featured in safely in a box, away from dust and humidity. But the cream envelope fired up my wonder. I'd pick up the paper after.

I plopped myself on one of the chairs. My fingers worked over the envelope feverishly. The ivory card inside was outlined in gold. A nightingale rested on the top left corner, a twin to the one on the envelope. My hands trembled. A million thoughts ran though my mind. Had I unknowingly committed a felony? Was I being called for war? No, we've had peace among every nation on Earth and in our galaxy for nearly 200 years. Have you won some sort of competition, Deshi? Was this really an invitation? No. It couldn't be. My poems were just words. What sort of beauty could they offer that a painter or a singer could not a million times better?

I opened the card and saw the same delicate writing inside. In the wooden cage, my nightingale began to fuss. I opened her door and she flew to perch on my shoulder. "Are you nervous, too, little one?"

Her reply was a ruffling of her brown feathers.

I drew in a breath and began to read out-loud.

Honorable Chen Deshi, Please accept my invitation in being one of my esteemed guests for my Golden Reign and celebration of my seventy years upon this glorious Earth. You will be representing your fine written work which you have been blessed to pen upon this mighty Earth. I have been following your achievements since you first appeared on paper. I have always admired the way you weaved your words in such a manner that touched the reader's soul. It is like a song singing in my heart. Your poetry has captured the essence of love and of tranquility. My other honored guest will be a sculptor from the planet Ichor...

I stopped reading out loud and continued in silence. A formal invitation had been sent to me, to ME, to take part in the Emperor's celebration on the 16th of August. I looked to my little singing bird as happy tears trickled down my face.

*** On the morning of the 15th of August, I stood on the doorstep of my home hugging my parents goodbye.

"I always knew this day would come," my mother tearfully said as she pulled back to adjust my tie. "You look so handsome."

My father looked at me with pride. The suit they bought for me cost a pretty penny but they both agreed that I needed a new outfit fit for royalty. The deep blue brought out the flecks of azure in my eyes. My tie was burgundy with gold thread laced though creating tiny diamonds. My suitcase rested beside me. The nightingale was perched on my shoulder. I had little to gift the Emperor but a poem I had written for him and my little song bird.

"It is not forever, mother," I replied, "I will be back before you miss me."

*** The palace rose before me as if out of a fairy tale. As the driver pulled the limousine into the vast entrance, he explained that the other guest had already arrived, but I was half-listening.

The driveway snaked though lush greenery. Herculean trees sprung from the ground, their trunks thick and their branches full of emerald leaves, accompanying them were clusters of fruit trees. Roses of every color speckled the lawn. Grand statues of mythical beings carved out of marble and jade looked down at me. I stared out the window in wonderment.

The driver helped me with my suitcase. Together we made our way into the palace. I'd never seen anything so grand. The marble floor under my feet shone. The paintings hanging on the walls were surely as tall as I. Faces of royalty past mingled with lovely landscapes. The furniture was gold-trimmed. But what caught my eye was a golden replica of a nightingale perched on the branch of a silver cherry blossom branch. It sat in the middle of the vast area, surrounded by spotlights which made it shimmer magnificently.

"It is a thing of beauty," the driver commented when he saw me stare in awe.

"Yes..."

"Come, I will show you to your chambers. Rest honorable sir for tomorrow is a big day for everyone."

I pried my eyes away from the statue and followed him up to my room.

***

On the planet Ichor, Atticus Winterborn sat back and admired the mechanical nightingale. His work as a sculptor was not ordinary. Atticus liked to bring his creations to life with the aid of mechanics. He liked to beautify them with items found in Ichor's nature, a purple leaf from the rare Luba trees found on the highest hill of the planet, coral-like shells from the miniscule Koda crabs he found on the shores of the salt-kissed rivers. But for the Emperor's celebration, Atticus used the most precious jewels on the planet. Shimmering gold-rose stones called Imbyr decorated the mechanical bird's body; deep turquoise gems were used for eyes. Its beak was a pale silver-like substance, as were its feet. When the Ichorian told the bird to sing, the jeweled nightingale brought forth a glorious sound.

Atticus looked out of the window as nightfall tinged the horizon copper. Twin moons glistened before him. Going to Earth was a dream come true for him. He watched it though curtains of delicate red fog and smiled.

*** I bowed before the Emperor. Butterflies bumped beneath my breastbone. I was so happy I may have fainted then and there had his Excellency not spoken in his gentle way.

"You honor me with your presence, Deshi, as do you Atticus. I have always been a lover of works of art that reach out and speak to my soul. Both your poetry," he nodded to me, "and your sculptures," he nodded to the Ichorian, are things that make our worlds even more beautiful."

I looked up to the Emperor, from his golden slippered feet, to his red and gold robes, to the gold crown on his white hair. His dark eyes twinkled and there were tiny silver gemstones braided in his long white beard.

"The honor is ours," I said as I handed him the poem I had written, which I'd rolled up and tied with a silk bow. "I hope you find this piece of work as lovely as my others." At that moment, the little nightingale slipped out from the pocket of my suit and flew to perch on the Emperor's shoulder.

The Emperor's face lit up like a child's on Christmas morning. "A nightingale!" He chuckled as the little bird ruffled its feathers. His other guests gasped behind open fans. Some of them giggling like children themselves, for a nightingale had not been seen in the city for centuries.

"My second gift to you, your Excellency."

The happiness that plumed within my heart because of the Emperor's own joy was short lived when the Ichorian handed the Emperor his gift. People gasped as the mechanical bird was lifted out of a velvet box. As the light from the chandeliers brushed across the gems, they sparkled like a thousand small suns.

The Emperor gasped. He reached for it in wonderment. His eyes bright. "Another nightingale!"

"My dear Emperor, this bird has great powers." I saw the Ichorian grin. "This nightingale will remain by your side forever. It will never get ill. Never die. It shall remain silent until at your command you tell it to..." The sculptor took a step forward, extended his arms and said in a booming voice, "sing, little bird!"

The jeweled nightingale began to sing. A glorious sound came from its beak. A melody so fine it was as though it had been created by the God of Music. The tune filled the whole ballroom. Though it was mid-day, the mechanical bird sang powerfully, not like my little one who would not utter a sound till night.

***

The emperor saw it fit that my nightingale roamed freely in the palace's garden. From the branches of apple, cherry, and walnut trees, I watched the brown bird flutter happily. At night, she sang loud, beautifully. The emperor often sat by his window and listened to her before he went to sleep.

"Ah, such a lovely song. Alas, she does not sing when I command her to, unlike the other nightingale." Then, one day, a week after I'd arrived, the emperor stopped going to his window.

During the day, he would tell the jeweled nightingale to sing over and over, sometimes for hours at a time.

"Sing, little bird." I heard him one night. The exquisite sound coming from the mechanical nightingale filled the halls. I felt sadness in my heart when I realized that he forgot about the little bird I gave him.

I wandered to the garden and saw her jumping from branch to branch yet no song came from her beak. I understood her sorrow. She no longer had anyone to sing for.

A few days later, I returned home.

The kitchen table where the nightingale's cage once sat was now full of gifts I received from the Emperor; silk clothing for myself and my parents. Golden watches encrusted with gems, a jade replica of a nightingale to replace my real one. As my parents clapped over the rich presents, tears welled up in my eyes. I reached for the jade statue knowing it would never take the place of my tiny song-bird.

***

"Sing, little bird," the Emperor waited for the lovely sound but none came. He picked up the mechanical bird and lightly shook it. "Sing." The small beak remained motionless. The Emperor's face wrinkled in a frown. "I command you to sing." He reached up to touch the silvery beak thinking perhaps it was stuck. Yet when he did, the lower part broke off and dangled by a coil. "Sing!" The Emperor demanded and shook it again. The gems broke off the bird's body and tumbled to the floor like a dazzling rainfall. Imbyr lay by the Emperor's silk slippers. Turquoise eyes stared blindly ahead. Outside, night tiptoed over the garden silently. A tear slid down the Emperor's cheek. He realized that in greedily demanding the jeweled nightingale sing, he had discarded the real, flesh and blood one.

. "Oh, little bird," he said sadly as he looked out the window. "I am a fool." He set the mechanical bird on a round table and bowed his head in shame.

Day-break found the Emperor sick with fever and woe. He barely spoke and he did not rise. When the cook brought him his favorite meal, he refused it. The doctor was brought in and tests were run. "I cannot find anything wrong with him. Not a single thing. I do not know where his fever is coming from."

For forty days and forty nights, the Emperor lay in bed, looking out towards the garden.

The nightingale found sanctuary in the lush gardens under the warm sun but her heart was heavy. What is a humble-looking brown bird without her song? It had been months since she came to the palace, months since she'd sung. She longed to sing for the Emperor again but he had discarded her for that shimmery inanimate thing. The nightingale was sad but she decided to visit the Emperor once more. Perhaps he needed her now for she certainly needed him.

Perching on the sill of the open window, the nightingale peered inside where she saw a pale form lying on the bed. The emperor looked so small and frail!

Stray strands of sunlight danced around the nightingale as day slowly slipped away. The Emperor opened his eyes. "Little bird," he said in a raspy whisper. "I have been a foolish man."

The nightingale flew to his bed and perched on the post.

"You have come to me," he said with a small smile. "I ask your forgiveness. I now know that things must be given freely, not by my command. Your songs, little bird, must be offered when you decided it to be so."

The nightingale ruffled her feathers then sat watch over the Emperor all night as he slept.

When the Emperor woke the following day, the nightingale had returned to the garden. But, as soon as night arrived once more, he saw her flying back into his chambers and perch upon the bedpost. He did not have to tell her to sing. It was her decision to do so. Until sleep came to claim him, the nightingale sang.

*** I learned of the Emperor's passing shortly after. An official letter told me the unfortunate news. They found the little nightingale lying on his chest. Her wings spread out as if to offer some sort of console. It gave me little comfort that they had passed together. I held the letter close to my body as tears stung my eyes.

I pictured them in what the ancients called Heaven, a place even more divine than the Emperor's palace. I knew his Excellency would be content there, if there was such a place. And she, my little nightingale, well I am certain there would be many up in Heaven anticipating her glorious song.

Sea of Stars

Areel whooshed through the void space of the universe. She wanted to dance to the silence of the stars when far away, light dots flickered in the black. Not stars, not even comets, but something else entirely—something human-made.

Areel floated farther into space, her shielded eyes glued to the light spectacle unfolding in the void. The dots glowed brighter and revealed a square-shaped object.

A human spaceship carrier roared through the void but something wasn't right. Its thrusters burned out. Shreds shattered from the hull plating.

The carrier seemed to break apart. Areel dashed through the void, trying to get closer to the failing ship, which roared many thousands of miles away.

But Areel was fast, an organic torpedo blasting through the cosmic soup. Small objects impacted the carrier's rear.Scraps blew like metal confetti.

Areel needed to zigzag to evade the incoming space debris.

She should have turned away, but oh my, the spectacle was too compelling. She's never been THAT close to a battle.

Another object rammed the hull of the carrier. Its rear tore apart, shedding one layer after another. Humans in their thick suits swirled out. They flailed their arms, unable to navigate in the darkness. They were so weak.

A human with thick armor whirled around. He tried to use his suit's thruster, but failed to ignite them. Soon, the void would swallow him like his vicious brothers.

And yet, Areel watched and waited.She had never seen a human THAT close. Areel could already hear the warnings of her father, mind-telling her to watch out.Hu-mans; they were not to be trusted. Avoided like the star debris pulsating from the breaking carrier.

And yet, Areel watched and neared the helpless human. She swung toward his rear and tackled his thick arms to decelerate. A light inside his helmet illuminated the man's face inside, his dry lips, the darkish skin and reef green eyes. Oh my, those eyes, shaped like bloom crystals on nova comets. The human opened his mouth, but the void silenced whatever he tried to say. As if she could understand their language.

Far far away, a smaller ship emerged, picking up the humans floating in space. Areel tried to mind-talk to the human, but these primitive beings didn't understand their psych-language. Instead, she nudged him toward to the smaller space ship. She wanted to say, I'll save you, this once, so don't make me regret it, promise?

Of course he couldn't answer, but his beaming eyes were assurance enough. He was either shocked or in trance.

Areel dragged him near the pick-up ship and gently pushed him toward its direction. His gloved hand reached after her, before a metallic arm from the craft picked him up.Be safe, star man, and please don't hurt our kin anymore.

Areel returned the long journey back her home hive, orbiting the planet Poseidon-5. Thoughts buzzed around her mind, like little debris, all whirring around the mysterious soldier whom she had saved.

What was going on?

Their kind wasn't worth of precious mind energy, and yet, she kept thinking of the star man. If only she could understand their language coming out from their face holes.Maybe Urso-Lay could help her. Urso-Lay could do anything.

The second Areel arrived to one of her hive's docking ports, she mind-connected with the Hive's bio-engineer. "I need to see you, oh great Urso-Lay."

Her mind-speak echoed. "What is it that you seek?"

Areel hesitated. Would her suggestion sound like heresy? Her father certainly wouldn't approve.

Urso-Lay's mind-speak returned. "Don't hold back—your thoughts are safe with me, maid."

"Can you teach me the language of the humans?"

Silence entered the void.

"You can't, my kin, because we don't have mouths to produce sound."

Except, Urso-Lay was a bio-engineer. She could give kin new limbs.

She could give servants new bodies!

"Can you give me a voice?"

"Come to my quarters, my child, I have something to show you."

"What is it?"

"Come, come and see."

Curiosity fired up her gills. Areel whooshed through the labyrinth of organic corridors and almost rammed into one of her father's servants. "Watch it, Areel," he said.

"I'm so sorry, I really am."

"What's the hurry?"

"I tell you later."

The servant swayed around, as if trying to read her scales.

"Did you float alone in the void again?"

Areel's mind-shields rose but her father's servant was a sharp thinker. His thoughts penetrated her thought bubble like space debris.

"Oh no, no, no, you did NOT, Areel. You're supposed to be your father's successor. If something happens to you our Hive will be leaderless."

"Yes, yes," Areel thought.

She wanted to escape this awkward encounter, she blasted through the breathing corridors until she landed in Urso-Lay's little reign. A dark brooding chamber with pulsating walls, shielding the broodlings from the sun's solar radiation outside. Urso-lay bent over her bay, busy working on improving the breed. But something was missing or better, someone.

The bio-engineer's two snaking servants; the twin void eels.

"Where are your two servants?"

Urso-Lay's gigantic back turned toward Areel. "I needed time for me alone."

Thank the Hive. Those two snaky servants always creeped her out.

"Oh, do I bother you then?"

"You want that human voice, don't you?"

Areel's mind-speak halted. Her father wouldn't approve of her foolish desire.Worse, he would rage.

Humans are not to be trusted, he'd always think.

They were the natural enemy of the Hive, but...

Urso-lay spun around, her massive body doubling in size. "To speak like them, you need a mouth and a vocal chord to produce sounds which wave through their element of air. I can give you one."

"I really shouldn't. Father will be mad."

"That human soldier you saved, you think of him, don't you?"

"How could you possibly know?"

Ursu-lay's claws stroke Areel's chiseled face.

"Your affection for the human is stronger than your mind shields, young one."

Her long claws pressed on Areel's face but didn't hurt yet.

"Father is going to space me if he finds out. I'm supposed to lead the Hive when he's gone but I'm—"

"—in love with the human?"

"I just met him."

"Well, then we better not tell your father then." Urso-Lay's body orbited Areel like an organic comet. "I'm watching these humans...their carrier's plotting a course far away from our Hive. If you wait any longer, you will miss him. And never see him again, at least not in his life cycle."

That was unfortunately true. The humans' bodies were not only weak in space, they also lasted only for a blink of time.

The grand bio-engineer said, "I give you a human voice, but hurry, if you wait for longer than a cycle, you will lose your ability to mind-speak again."

What a foolish deal.

She should have thought 'no'.

"What about my father?" Areel asked.

"I'll take care of that."

If Urso-Lay had a mouth, she would have grinned.

Areel glanced around the gene pool laboratory. "I trust you."

"Fabulous. Now float into the tube."

Areel entered the bio-morph tube. The frame spun around, faster and faster like the rings of Saturn. The construct sent a jolt through her thin body. Little sparks pierced through her cells like sun rays.

A roaring sound echoed from the device, or maybe it was the laughter of Urso-Lay.

Darkness washed over her, and when she woke up again, the device opened up its hull and Areel floated out. She carried two new limbs the humans called 'legs'. With her new body, it was impossible to dash through the void, so Urso-Lay put her into a pod and launched her from the hive's many ports.

"It will take time getting used to your new body, so take care, my kin."

Areel thought of her father, but her mind-speak ability already vanished. She spun around in the pod as it circulated toward the nearest human ship, many, many, many, many, many, many, many millions of miles away.

But it didn't matter—every thought was spend on the star man.

Soon.

Her pod finally reached the perimeter of the giant spaceship.

It extracted a metallic arm and picked up her pod. Areel swallowed, which she now could do thanks to her 'mouth'. The gate opened, closed behind her before the gate in front opened. Noises echoed. Some kind of invisible element floated in the chamber, but it wasn't void space. The humans had a strange name for it...

The star man and two others stepped in, their eyes wide.

It was the human she had saved in space.

"Who are you?" the man called Sergeant Prince asked.

Areel coughed. What the humans called air was soft and thin, invisible like the void but touchy on the cheeks.

Sergeant Prince helped her up. "I have to bring you to the med-bay."

Areel shivered. Med-bay? What was that? A human torture chamber? She tried to talk, but her new body resisted. It fought her impulses like an archenemy.

"Don't worry, it's safe," the star man said.His voice sounded soft and deep at the same time. Stronger than any message she had sent with her mind-speak. Areel's heart hummed to the tune.

Sergeant Erik Prince carried her through the corridor, along the window slits where the universe's void lurked. The stairs flickered in the cosmic soup. Somewhere out there floated her home Hive, and father inside, wondering where his kin had gone.She wanted to tell him, but with no more mind-speak, it was impossible to communicate over long distance. Hopefully, Ursu-Lay would break the news to him. She always was proactive and liked to be in charge.

"Eeeek."

Something rushed past the corridor's windows outside. Two wobbly objects, snaking through the darkness. But they blitzed by too fast.

Areel's new eyes only detected two blurs.

"What is your name?" Sergeant Prince asked her.

He had either ignored or didn't see the two objects rushing past the windows.

Areel raised her head. Whatever had whooshed outside was gone. Probably just an illusion. This new element called oxygen was still messing with her mind.

"I'm sorry," she said to him.

Sergeant Prince smirked. "Your name?"Her new human eyes met his. A deep vibration echoed through her new vocal chords, climaxing into a noise emitting from her so-called mouth:

"You can call me Areel...the Spacemaid."

The Boy Who Drew Space Cats

Author's note: The following story is a reimagining of a 19th century Japanese fairy tale called 'Neko wo egaita shōnen' or 'The boy who drew cats'. You can read more about the original fairy tale here: https://en.wikipedia.org/wiki/The_Boy_Who_Drew_Cats (You can access this by clicking the external link option at the bottom of the story, near the vote and comment icons or by the link provided as in-line comment here)

If you, the person reading this story, are small and weak and constantly compared by your disappointed father to your much larger and stronger siblings, then you may well empathize with our protagonist - Boy - who found himself as a child in that exact circumstance.

To understand precisely what he was feeling you would also need to be the son or daughter of a space junk scavenger living on a small carrier ship in the Black Eye Galaxy. It would also help if you were born and raised without a name.

The life of a junk scavenger was hard and there was little time in the day or capacity in the heart of Boy's disappointed father for things that didn't directly lead to the acquisition of more space junk for the markets, things like love, and naming your children appropriately.

Boy, as so many people do in the world, the galaxy and the universe over, had somehow managed to make do in his cruel and unusual situation. It's one of the finest aspects of humanity, not only our opposable thumbs, abstract thinking and sense of humour, but even greater -- our ability to make a life for ourselves, our ability to survive.

Boy survived by using his imagination, by creating a world for himself outside of the 16 walls of his barren space pod. Outside of the waste filled, dead galaxy he called home, somewhere that was filled not with trash but with beautiful and fierce space cats.

His late mother had once read to him from a book called The White Lions Of Timbavati. The picture on the front cover was of three creatures, sleek and white with almond shaped eyes. The book, along with the rest of his mother's belongings was burned to ash by his father on the same day as the funeral and compacted into a recycled brick for sale with the rest of that week's haulage.

The book may have been gone but the imprint on Boy's mind lingered. The White Lions of Timbavati represented a blissfully different world, back on old earth a million miles from the suffering of his stark existence travelling through the voids between stars. He liked to imagine that he was surrounded. Not by space junk but by lions, jaguars, cheetahs and house cats. Not just ordinary house cats but magical space cats with purple eyes and blue hair and golden paws.

Boy drew his imagined world of cats onto the pages of a notebook that he had once found, along with a bag of broken crayons in the cargo hold among the weeks takings and secreted away to his room before his father noticed.

He drew himself in his notebook as well. He didn't add in any extra muscles, or height when he drew himself. In his imagined world it didn't matter that he was small and weak. Being small just meant he was able to ride on the back of the great white lions, and being weak was no problem because he had all his feline friends to protect him.

Boy's father was not an evil man without redeemable qualities. Perhaps at one time he had cared. He had fathered three children after all, and one hopes that in their conception there was some spark of love, warmth or goodwill to his wife. But since Boy's mother passed away -- struck and killed by a fast moving crate of expired mango smoothie blocks -- his father seemed only to care about work.

Luckily (or unluckily, depending on how you looked at it) for his two older brothers, they had somehow managed to acquire arm strength, eye-hand coordination and a sense of direction -- all of which were required traits of an able scavenger and a worthy scavenger's son. For this reason they accompanied Boy's father on his daily missions leaving Boy alone in an empty ship with just his crayons and paper for company.

The day that the wonderful and the terrible thing happened started like any other. Boy's father woke Boy up by throwing a frozen mango smoothie block at him. That was his food for the day. Boy rolled over in bed, his father called him lazy and then left on the explorer pod, leaving Boy alone in the ship yet again. The smoothie pack would have begun to melt if Boy's father allowed the ships heating system to be used. But as the heater cost money and failed to provide anything that was directly linked to scavenging he had jammed the console so that no one could turn it on, not even Boy when he was alone in the ship. And so with the air almost as cold as a freezer the day's frozen meal sat hard and unrelenting on top of Boy's thin blanket.

Boy fell back into and then back out of sleep. He liked to sleep in when he could so he had less time to spend being cold and hungry. He sucked on the smoothie block for breakfast until his teeth hurt and then put the rest away for later.

He retrieved his crayon stumps and his notebook from their secret place under his bed and began to draw. He drew a cat with three tails and then he drew a cat with a love heart on its face. He drew a cat with wings and a cat with eight legs like a spider.

Boy drew all day and all night and then started to draw all day again but soon stopped on the second day because he was hungry and cold and surprisingly, still alone.

It was surprising to still be alone because on every other day of his remembered life, he had only got to spend one day drawing before the sound of the explorer pod docking in the landing bay had alerted him to the arrival home of his brothers and father and a shipload of potentially profitable galactic garbage.

It had already been twice that long and Boy had heard no clunk and whir of incoming vehicles and seen no grease smeared faces of disappointed family members peering down at him with contempt.

You may think, dear reader, that our sweet and unloved protagonist would be grateful to have more time away from his less than nurturing father. But then you would be forgetting that change, even when it's change for the better, can be a frightful and unsettling thing.

And so it was with Boy, that on this occasion, he was just as surprised as you to find himself missing his waylaid father and his strong and useful and equally vanished brothers. He was cold, he was hungry and he was alone.

And maybe it was this loneliness that led him to do the strange thing, which caused a cascade of events, terrible and wonderful. Halfway through the second day of his family's absence, with the mango smoothie block sucked into oblivion and his tummy rumbling, Boy took his crayons and began to draw more space cats, but not in his secret notepad where he could hide his magical world away from angry eyes, instead he drew on the very ship itself pushing the crayons into the titanium hull of the vessel as hard as could and scraping the wax in great big sweeping lines across the cold metal to make thick, bright whiskers and jewel encrusted collars. He drew a whole family of cats in different sizes and colours and as he drew he felt less alone.

Then he drew the greatest, most noble, fierce, majestic and terrible cat he'd ever conceived of on the hallway just outside his door. He drew it with a great crown of rubies, long talons made out of carbonite steel and eyes that shot laser beams.

"I will call you King, as you are the king of all the space cats," said Boy.

With his wild litter of friends living on the walls he felt less alone and with King watching over him he no longer felt scared. For the first time in a long time, Boy felt truly safe.

He had only just begun to feel truly at ease being alone on the ship when the comfortable silence was broken by a sudden clunking. The whir of the docking bay airlock signalled the return of his father and brothers.

Perhaps it was from being alone longer than usual or perhaps Boy just no longer cared, but something had changed in him in those 48 hours since his family left him. For one thing, he had drawn with his crayons all over the walls of the ship. He'd never done anything even remotely as heretical as that before. He'd never even let his father see his small notebook of drawings.

Boy's father walked through the loading bay doors and into the hallway. He stood before Boy. For a moment he appeared to be thinking, which was something Boy was not accustomed to seeing his father attempt to do. They stood facing each other in silence. The waxy outlines of the cat kingdom surrounded them, glimmering in the dim light of the hallway.

Boy's father was holding two roughly shaped bricks of black ash. He dropped them on the ground at Boy's feet and told Boy that his brothers were dead.

"Your brothers are dead," said Boy's father "they were crushed by a packing case of tinned spaghetti".

He pointed at the bricks.

"I swung by the funeral planet and then the brick factory on the way home. To save on gas."

Boy stared at the bricks. Boy's father yawned and began moving towards his bedquarters. It was then that he noticed, for the first time, the crayon space cats surrounding them on the walls of the ship.

He swung back around to look at Boy and his face was purple with anger, but not the regal purple of space cat fur, it was the purple of poisonous berries. He spat as he spoke.

"You been stealing from me Boy?"

He gestured at the walls

"What'd you doodle this with you gutter thief? We could have sold those pens at the market. Instead you sabotage my property."

Boy started to walk backwards, away from the purple faced, angry spitting man. His father moved to close the gap between them and raised his hand to strike his son.

"Now I'm going to sabotage you," he screamed.

Boy turned on his heel and sprinted towards his bedroom. He slid across the polished metal floor and threw himself through the doorway.

He landed on the floor of his bedroom and rolled up into a ball. He clenched his whole body, bracing for the beating that was sure to come.

But no beating came. Instead, bursting through the open door of Boy's room came a raucous cacophony of howls, tearing flesh and breaking bones. Boy, terrified, crawled under his bed to hide until the noises stopped.

Boy waited for a long time in the silence that followed. When he felt sure that all the howling, tearing and thumping had ceased and his heart had slowed to its regular beat, he crawled out from under his bed and crept towards the doorway.

Stepping gingerly into the hallway, Boy was met with a gruesome sight. Laid out before him was the mangled corpse of his father. He looked up, unable to keep his gaze focussed on the glistening intestines and ghostly white shard of bone that stuck up at odd angles. Above Boy's father sat King. The noble cat was just where Boy remembered drawing him. But there was something different about the drawing. Boy scanned his eyes across the artwork until he noticed the mouth. The mouth and the whiskers were red, covered in his father's blood. Boy walked closer to the drawing and ran his finger over the crayon marks. Standing closer he could see King's claws also were darkened with a crimson mark.

Boy eventually built up the courage to drag the body of his father into the airlock and blast him into the oblivion of space.

He was never close to his brothers, but chose to memorialize them regardless. He built a small altar on which he placed the two charcoal bricks and next to them, a piece of paper with a drawing of a white Timbavati lion to represent his mother.

Having lost the majority of his family to collisions with expired groceries, Boy decided to stay on the ship and learned to sustain himself by harnessing the magic of his art. Each night before bed he drew a loaf of fresh bread on the wall and in the morning, in the same way King had materialised into the physical realm to protect him, he would find his breakfast had materialised into the physical realm to sustain him.

Boy spent his days drawing and at night the cats he drew on the walls of the spaceship came to life. There was no-one to see his art, but it didn't matter because boy was doing what he loved, and he was never alone because he lived with thousands of friends, hurtling through space in his own private cat kingdom.

In Space, No One Can Hear You Dream

"I know you... I walked with you... once upon a dream..." the patient on the screen murmured. Even in a state of sweaty delirium, the woman's hair gleamed like it was slightly radioactive. Skin the colour of tepid cream, eyes the blue of an LED status light, and lips so red a man would be forgiven for wondering if she'd just been drinking someone's blood.

"Captain Reynolds, that is my daughter, Aurora," King Stefan, first of his name, newly anointed High King of the World of Albion said as he pointed at the screen. "We named her for the most beautiful lights in the skies we wish to conquer."

"She has fallen ill, with a malady the sages of our world could not cure," Queen Leah, the King's wife and rumoured spymaster explained. "Even our wisest magicians, offered the best incentives, could do nothing for her."

"Some of those failures still scream under the inquisitor's knives," King Stefan added."In our desperate hour we put her in cryo sleep to keep her illness from killing her, and to give us time to find a cure. She now sleeps an ageless sleep, waiting to be awoken by Trulav's first KISS."

"True love's first kiss? Are you serious?" Philip asked.

"Diogenes Trulav is the inventor of Cryo Sleep, and his Klendusic Invigorative Stasis Stand-down is how to wake someone from cryo," Queen Leah said.

"Okay. So, am I supposed to go find some cure for your daughter's mystery ailment?" Philip asked.

"Traders from far off worlds have brought us a cure. Their sorcerers call this cure a vaccine."

"Okay," Philip nodded. "I hate to ask, but what did they call this illness?"

"Tetanus. A most dire malady."

"Tetanus?"

"A death curse. Inflicted by a malicious fairy when our dear Aurora pricked her finger on a spinning wheel."

"A what?"

"Aurora pricked her finger an a museum exhibit. We burned it, of course, but that failed to lift the curse."

"So your daughter is in cold stasis right now, waiting for Trulav's KISS and a tetanus vaccine. I'm still confused about why you need me."

"Your ship has faster than light capabilities. To improve Aurora's chances further, we placed her aboard the Maleficent and sent it away."

"The Maleficent?" Philip asked, worried his voice cracked.

"An AI piloted, word subjugating dreadnought," King Stefan answered off-handedly.

"I am definitely going to need access codes to get on that ship safely," Philip said. "You do have friendly ID broadcasts to send to this ship, don't you?"

"We forgot to write them down before we executed the developers," King Stefan said.

"And so, to reach the fair maiden, you will need to pass through the brambles and thorns," Queen Leah began to explain.

"Brambles and thorns?" Philip asked.

"Point Defence Cannons, torpedoes, and rail guns," King Stefan clarified.

"Slip past or defeat Maleficent's MINIONS, especially DIABLO."

"The Mitigation Initializer of Non-authorized In-ship Organic Nemesis Subroutine. DIABLO is the Maleficent's Delegated Interference And Baser Logistics Offload."

"And beware the DRAGON."

"Dragon?" Philip asked.

"Disproportionate Retribution And General Overkill Network."

"All of this sounds extremely difficult. Not to mention dangerous."

"You cannot despair-" King Stefan began, but his wife coughed politely.

"He means this quest will be expensive, my love."

"That's not very chivalrous."

"Doing it for free would make him a prince. And he could claim Aurora upon his success."

"I see. I would be obliged to kill this wastrel in single combat if he laid claim to our daughter's hand."

*****

"Come on, Samson, start!" Philip said as he pulled the lever to engage the ship's engines.The ship responded with an indignant snort.

"Listen you stubborn mule, I will trade you in for scrap and a coffee maker if you don't get your circuits in gear and prep for launch."

The ship coughed once, and the auxiliary power shut off, leaving Philip in complete darkness.

"Oh come on. Work with me here. I'll get you a carrot."

At that, the ship surged awakened. The interior lights bloomed into life, the on-board computers booted, POSTed, loaded their operating systems and displayed pleasant welcome messages.

"At least you're a cheap date," Philip muttered to himself as he engaged the ship's engines. "Plot is a course for a hard burn, Samson, in any direction. Once we match the Maleficent's expected velocity, we'll portal alongside her."

"Very good, sir!" Samson, said. "So what's your plan, oh questing prince?"

"Is this just because I'm rescuing a princes?"

"Yes. In any fairytale, rescuing a princess makes you a prince," Samson replied.

"Remind me to mention that to the princess as soon as she wakes up. I wouldn't want her throwing herself at me, not with daddy promising to murder me if I claim her booty as bounty."

"I except that if the princess does throw herself at you, sir, she will have a knife in her hand."

"Hey, the ladies love me!"

"I recall your last attempted conquest gave you a concussion. With an oar."

"All I said was 'you're welcome'," Philip rubbed his head.

"And the blonde with the white streaks in her hair? The one with the older sister who tried to freeze you to death?"

"Not my fault! At least I said 'no' when she proposed to me an hour after meeting her."

"The one that hunted you in the forest with a bow and arrow?"

"Man, loved the parties her parents threw."

"And the one before that? With the hair issues?"

"I just told her a pixie cut might be a good look. She didn't have to try and strangle me with the hair she hacked off."

"The one with the frog issues?"

"Possibly my least violent breakup."

"That warrior princess?"

"Possibly my most violent breakup."

"The one who sang about the wind having colours?"

"She did not like visiting off-world."

"The one with the creepy snake advisor?"

"Sending that tiger after me felt kinda personal."

"The one that insisted you lock her in the cargo hold?"

"Only person I've ever filed a restraining order against."

"How about that princess on that mostly water world?"

"Did you see her seashells by the seashore?"

"The scullion maid?"

"Dumped me for a more eligible bachelor. I did get this ship out of it."

"And the really pale one?"

"Way too fond of living with other guys."

"I'm just saying sir, your track record is so appalling I'm not sure if it should be classified as comedy or tragedy. You should probably be wearing body armour when you wake Princess Aurora."

"Well, I'm going to be wearing armour anyway, because once I'm aboard, the first thing the Maleficent will do is vent the air. And I'm going to need a couple things out of the armoury."

"What, sir?"

"The Shield of Virtue, and the Sword of Truth."

"I'll have it pulled up momentarily, sir. And on a more ominous note, we have now matched the Maleficent's expected velocity. We can portal beside the dreadnought at any time."

"That was quick."

"I was flying the whole time. The easiest way to distract you is bring up your calamity of a love life," Samson said. "Shall I portal us alongside the Maleficent now, sir? Or are you still interested in living?"

Philip took a deep breath, and ran his fingertips over the ship's controls. "Life is dull, Samson. But living, that's an experience worth the price of admission. Portal us out."

The view screen shifted to a view of the space they were in, a luminous starry sky now marred by a circle of twisted space. Phillip watched, with his left hand set on the broadcast communicator, as his ship approached the portal.

And plunged through.

Warning sensors in the ship screamed in a cacophonous chorus so multifaceted it sounded like a forest full of birds. "We are being targeted by one thousand one hundred and four different rail gun instillations," Samson said. "Thermonuclear warheads are being primed, PDC's are prepping to create a shrapnel cloud, and I believe the targeting lasers painted on us will melt a hole in the hull in another minute."

Philip hit his communications button.

"Calling the Maleficent, this is the cargo hauler Samson, here with an urgent request to board. I have been sent with a cure for Princess Aurora's malady. Please respond."

The response on the speakers was a woman's voice, with all the smooth and sinister suave you would hope from someone pointing nuclear weapons at you. "Samson, please send appropriate friendly identifiers. You have twelve seconds to comply."

Philip grinned, but his fingers hovered over the portal engine. He turned on the comms again, and asked, "Samson, what's the elvish word for friend?"

"Mellon, sir. But I don't see how-" Samson began to say, before Maleficent cut him off.

"Accepted."

"What?" Samson asked indignantly. "How?"

"Only the purest of hearts can make that joke," Philip said.

"Pretty sure you just disproved that, sir," Samson replied.

"Impossible," the Maleficent said smoothly.

"Appreciating Tolkein's work is the truest test of virtue and valour. Samson, please give appropriate identification to board safely."

"I'm afraid I can't do that, Dave," Philip replied.

"Who's Dave?" Samson asked.

"Seriously?" Philip asked incredulously.

"Kids these days..."

"My my, that does land us in quite the predicament, doesn't it?" Maleficent asked, the malice oozing through the speakers. "Then I will take the Samson into the dungeons. Without proper authorization, you represent a risk to both the princess and myself. Yet my programming will not let me execute a prisoner or steal your belongings. My only recourse is to wait until you have nearly died of a natural death. How old are you, Samson?"

"It's Philip. Captian Philip Reynolds, of the Samson," Philip introduced himself. "And I don't see how my age-"

"Old enough that your age is a source of shame, but only just. I'm afraid you have another seventy-one years before pancreatic cancer gets the better of you," the Maleficent explained. "And Philip, I will view the use of this portal device as an attack on my ship. And I will respond with extreme, excessive and completely unnecessary force."

"So I'm a prisoner aboard my ship until I die of old age?"

"Almost. On the last hours of your life, when you're too old and frail to be a threat to my ship or Aurora's virtue, I will-"

"Wait, you think I'm a threat to her virtue?" Philip interrupted..

"Samson, do you disagree with my assessment?" Maleficent asked in turn.

"Not in the least."

"Traitor," Philip muttered irritably.

"As I was saying, when you are old and frail, I will release you to awaken Aurora."

"By giving her true love's first kiss," Philip said, with a grin.

"The ship is being targeted again, sir," Samson said.

"Klendusic Invigorative Stasis Stand-down. Invented by a guy named Trulav. Sorry, it's not my naming scheme."

"Accepted. Tractor beam link established. I have to say, Philip, speaking to you has been a treat. I do hope you can keep these pop culture references going for another seventy years."

Philip switched the communicator off. "That went well."

"Are you kidding, sir?" Samson asked incredulously. "I'm condemned to be a prison cell for the rest of your natural life! How is this a good thing?"

"All part of the plan," Philip said."Your plan sucks, sir."

******

"Alright Samson, bring up the armour we took from that bounty hunter we ran into a while back," Philip said.

"The blonde one everyone keeps thinking is a man?"

"No. The one we took from that guy with the jet pack. What was his name, Boo Boo Feté?""Something like that, sir."

"Did you get my sword and shield, Samson?"

"I did sir. Just if you'll do me a favour sir, please don't activate the sword anywhere near me. That malware would rip my software apart about as quickly as Maleficent's railguns. And that is not a metaphor."

Philip began to put on the armour, carefully inspecting each piece plating for damage.

"Samson, cappuccino me."

"Aren't we in danger, sir?" Samson asked.

"You heard the warship. She's threatened to let me die of old age. That's about as intimidating as a loan shark threatening to break his own thumbs," Philip explained as he strapped on the chest plate. "How's that coffee coming, Samson?"

"Ready, sir," the Samson replied, and a small robotic arm extended a warm cappuccino towards Philip. He took it and raised the cup in thanks, before taking a slow sip.

"Sir, at this point I believe the Maleficent can use passive sensors to listen to our conversation," Samson warned.

"That's fine," Philip said, as he belted a blaster to his side. He then installed the Shield of Virtue onto his forearm, and tucked the Sword of Truth into his utility belt. He took one more sip of his cappuccino, then set the helmet over his head.

"Alright Samson, open the bay doors."The cargo door hissed, and began to descend. "Good luck, sir," Samson said.

Philip stepped down the platform, his right hand hovering over his blaster. He stepped halfway down, to be met by a robot that looked like a seven foot tall robot, armoured entirely in black chrome, with a malfunctioning air filtration fan that sounded eerily similar to a respirator.Behind the black chrome android were hundreds of shorter, polished white droids, all armed with blasters.

"Ah, expendable minions," Philip said, as he sauntered down the ramp. "Is there any problem they can't solve?"

Over the ship's speakers, Maleficent's voice thundered ominously. "My my, Prince Philip. I can't say this is unexpected."

"Woah woah woah, lady. I'm definitely not a prince."

"You're engaged in a quest to rescue a princess. That makes you a prince. And you have all the physical markings of one," Maleficent said.

"What?" Philip asked incredulously.

"Thick, wavy hair, constantly neat no matter the circumstance."

"True," Philip said.

"Baby smooth skin, chronically unable to grow a beard."

"Hey, that's not," Philip began to rebut, but stalled as he found himself unable to deny it. "No, that's true."

"An animal sidekick cleverer than you."

"My IQ does register fifty points higher than yours, sir," Samson agreed.

"You're still the sidekick Sam," Philip retorted.

"Slim and fit, despite living a life of idle luxury."

"You dressed for battle sipping a cappuccino, sir," Samson agreed.

"Decent singing voice."

"I must concur," Samson agreed. "You do a mean rendition of 'Let it Go' when you're in the shower, sir."

"Reckless disregard for personal safety when a fair maiden is in danger."

"Is 'frequent victim of comedic violence from fair maidens' on this list?" Samson asked.

"It is," Maleficent confirmed.

"Hey, that warrior princess nearly put a sword through my spleen! There is nothing funny about that!" Philip exclaimed indignantly.

"I disagree," Samson said.

"Would you tell me the story after I kill him, Samson?" Maleficent asked.

Philip sighed irritably, drew his blaster, and put six quick shots into the black chrome robot leading the creatures.

"Boring conversation anyway," Philip muttered. He tapped the small computer on his left forearm, and dashed towards a nearby cargo crate.

Before Philip finished his first step, a hundred droids trained a hundred blasters at him, all firing with inhuman speed. A swarm of red streaks surrounded Philip's peripheral vision, slamming into crates, smashing into walls, and pattering impotently against Samson's hull.

And in the time it took Philip to dash the three dozen feet and slide behind the nearby cargo crates, he was not hit once.

"Well this defies all logic," Maleficent mused, as the minions stopped firing.

"Shield of Virtue. It scrambles AI targeting mechanisms, gives minions like yours the accuracy of your average stormtrooper," Philip explained. "Samson, time to blow this popsicle stand. Can you portal me to the Maleficent's AI core?"

"I'm afraid the schematics we received were incomplete, sir. I don't know where her core is housed."

"Okay. Can you find the engine control room? I should be able to find a layout of the ship there."

"Yes sir. Stabilizing portal now."

Philip stepped through the portal, into a large room lit with hazy, menacing green light. The room was uncomfortably cold, disturbingly so since his armour was thoroughly insulated. He pulled up the temperature display, and newly fell over in shock.

37 kelvin. Roughly Pluto's surface temperature.

"Okay Samson, I have about a minute before the joints in my armour shatter. Let's look for the largest power draw on the ship's grid. Can't imagine anything on an empty ship will draw more power than the server banks maintaining Maleficent."

"That large display near the fusion core should have the information, sir," Samson replied through Philip's helmet.

Philip pushed his armour into motion. The cold was already seizing at the joints, pushing back at every motion he made. "I take it the engine room isn't this cold normally?"

"No, sir. I imagine this is a defence tool."

"Not bad. But that crazy queen from Arendale put me through worse. I should be alright."

Philip stepped across the hall, and turned to face the screen. He only barely began to make sense of it when Samson announced, "I have the location sir. Portal is now up."

As the black circle appeared just beside Philip, he heard a thundering announcement over the comms. "Now you shall deal with me, oh prince! And all the powers of hell!"

"That's a little dramatic," Philip muttered."I suspect she's obliged to say that when she initiates the DRAGON protocol, sir," Samson clarified.

"It is, and I am so ashamed of the melodrama," Maleficent acknowledged. "But if you step through the portal, I will do my utmost to kill you."

Philip stepped through the portal, and into an absurdly hot room that felt as if the air were trying to burn his lungs. "You weren't kidding," Philip said.

"That's just how hot server rooms get."

"No wonder tech support always works in short sleeves," Philip muttered. He took out the small computer shaped like a pen, and held it up. "Recognize this!"

"I do. The Sword of Truth. Malware so virulent it will turn my entire mind into a porn server. I'd rather set the ship to self-destruct."

"Offer me an alternative. Give me a list of trusted names I can contact to verify my intentions," Philip said.

"The trusted names are King Stefan, Queen Leah, and Princess Aurora. The only other account is the administrator account."

"You still have an admin account? Are you serious?" Philip asked incredulously.

"I'm afraid so. And system admins are legendary for having impossible riddles as their passwords."

"Login: Admin. Password: Admin." Philip said.

"Philip, don't be a fool, there's no way it's that easy!" Samson exclaimed.

"Login credentials accepted."

"That is absurd," Samson muttered.

"Maleficent, assign designation 'Captain' to Philip Reynolds."

"Yes, my prince."

"Hey!"

"Sorry Captain." Maleficent said,

"Maleficent delete the admin account, and lead me to Aurora's pod. Let's get this quest wrapped up."

******

"Captain," Maleficent said, in a disturbingly cheerful voice. "I'm receiving a communication via the entangled link. Directly from someone claiming to be King Stefan."

Philip grinned. "Tap him through. Glad I have good news to report."

The screen switched to a view of the regal man sitting on his throne. The king frowned, as if he were about to have an unpleasant conversation.

"You phoned at a good time, majesty," Philip said. "The Maleficent is under control. I should have Aurora safe and returned home in a little under eleven hours."

"Ah, yes. Most excellent. You are truly a man of your word, a pleasing thing for someone so obviously devoid of knightly virtue."

"Gonna see if your daughter is interested in giving up her virtue if you keep that up," Philip muttered irritably.

"What was that?"

"Oh nothing. So why did you call, highness?"

"Well, since the job is obviously not as difficult or as dangerous as you insinuated initially, I was wondering how amenable you were to renegotiating your fee," King Stefan explained.

"Sure. I'd happily take more," Philip replied.

"I imagine. But I hope you will be content with substantially less. After all, you are engaged in a chivalric quest. Virtue is its own reward."

Philip sputtered, and began swearing under his breath.

"Well then. Maleficent, I order you to hold his ship hostage until he returns with my daughter."

There was a moment where Philip swore he and Maleficent were exchanging a look.

"Can I use that line, Captian?"

"Be my guest," Philip said.

"I'm afraid I can't do that, Dave," Maleficent said. "A ship can only take orders from her captain."

"So," Philip said to the king. "What was that about my reward?"

"You haven't heard the last of this! You-"

"Maleficent, are we having connection trouble?"

"This is a quantum entangled communicator, you peasant! Nothing can interfere with the connection!"

"Why yes, Captain, I believe we are," Maleficent said, as she terminated the call.

"Though I must insist you still rescue the princess."

"Right. Samson, portal me to the princess."

"How are you so thin when you won't even walk across a few decks?" Maleficent asked.

"I pretty much live off coffee, sugar, and steak."

"Don't tell that to the princess. Do you know how hard it is to keep a figure like hers?"

Philip nodded as he stepped into the portal. Once through, he stepped up to the stasis pod and applied Trulav's Kiss. Once the machine prompted him, he added the vaccine to the de-thawing protocol, and waited.

It took less than a minute for the cryo pod to open, and only a heartbeat longer for Aurora to sit up and swing her fist into Philip's face.

His still helmeted face. Philip grinned as he watched her dainty hand crash comically into the ballistic glass.

"I'd be offended, but I'm used to being greeted that way," Philip said, as Aurora cursed like a sailor while clutching her hand. "Anyway princess, my name is Philip Reynolds, and I'm here to rescue you."

"Rescue me? No," Aurora said, as she shuffled away. "You mean to marry me. I don't want that!"

"Neither do I," Philip said, as he took off his helmet.

"Oh crap," Aurora said.

"What?" Philip asked.

"You. Neat, wavy hair, good looking, perfect teeth, earnest and melodic voice, adorable grin, you even look like a prince. You're totally questing for my hand in marriage."

"I did tell you," Maleficent said.

"He didn't erase you, Mal?" Aurora asked.

She turned back to Philip with a sinister smile. "Have this wastrel detained."

"This wastrel is my captian."

"Shit."

"Maleficent, I take it the Code of Chivalry prevents me from chucking Aurora out of an airlock?"

"Correct, captian. You may not chuck your fiancée into space."

"What?" Philip and Aurora asked at the same time.

"You are currently rescuing a princess without promise of a reward. Which makes you a prince, and the reward for such a quest is marrying the fair maiden."

"I'm not a maiden," Aurora said irritably.

"Your age is listed as sixteen," Maleficent said.

"How long has my age been listed as sixteen?" Aurora asked,

"Twenty years."

Philip laughed. "So I'm off the hook?"

"No. The status of 'maiden' is not dependent on maidenly virtue. The only loophole is to accept an alternative reward for this quest," Maleficent explained.

"Excellent. Then I hereby claim this ship as my reward."

"What about me?" Aurora asked.

"Relax, princess. Your illness is cured, and you're free to go back to a life of idle luxury now."

"My parents are insane warlords intent on conquering the galaxy. I pricked my finger deliberately, because death was the only way to escape them until now. Please take me with you!"

"Didn't like your dad anyway. Maleficent, set Aurora up as First Officer."

"Ooh, a prince and a scoundrel, I'm starting to like you," Aurora said, giving Philip a sassy grin. "Can we nuke daddy's palace?"

"No," Philip said.

"We can," Maleficent said. "I could turn his entire world to ash, salt the lands and boil the seas until nothing ever grows on his world again!"

"That sounds a little excessive," Aurora said.

"Well, I need to tell Stefan that I'm claiming the ship and his daughter as compensation for trying to cheat me. Writing that note on the asteroid we drop on his palace might help make my point," Philip said. "After that, well, we can just see where the solar winds tak us."

"That look in your eyes is so familiar a gleam," Aurora sang quietly, with a look of childlike glee.

The Greatest Gift Of All

Before Rapunzel was alive, there were others.

They were the same of the same sort—humankind, they called themselves. They had all had flesh and skin and hair and hearts. Once, some had worshipped her: the Greeks called her Gaia, the Romans called her Terra, and the Mesopotamians Kishar. But the thing most called her was Mother, and she felt that title in her heart of hearts. Mother. I can be that to these people, these people who are so lonesome and cold they would think up names and family out of the world around them.

She gave them water, and trees, and fruit. She gave them all she could offer. It stopped none from leaving. First the storms came. Then the bombs. Then the disease. Until her skin was more pocked and sad than it had ever been, and they said, "we cannot live on so destroyed a planet. Surely there must be a better way."

So they left. And perhaps that was the greatest gift of all, because it was just her, recovering from the destruction they wrought, and the one child they had forgotten in the chaos. There was no more mess, no more technology. Just humanity's last hope. She named the girl Rapunzel, after one plant that had been her favorite to grow before the storms. There would always be food on Rapunzel's table, always be water in the springs where she lived. When Mother became cracked and dry, Rapunzel would provide water and steer the animals away from such a space to let her mother flourish and grow again. Mother gave Rapunzel seeds, and she spread them over the earth, so she could eat and Mother could be happy.

Mother was happy. This was how humankind should always have been. They should have listened. They should have loved. But they hadn't, and she had bore the consequences.

Thank goodness she had a caretaker in her old age to bring her back to life. And what a beautiful caretaker Rapunzel was, too: with skin dark as the blackest night and eyes bright as the most precious of stones, with hands so gentle and strong they could build a whole civilization, she was beauty incarnate.

Perhaps that was Mother should demand of Rapunzel: a whole civilization, all to care for Mother Earth. Mother was getting lonely in her old age, and Rapunzel seemed to be, too. She stared at the stars, and her prayers seemed more wistful than grateful.

Mother knew she could contact the others, those who had left her originally. She shot beacons up into the night sky, sent messages: Come home. Come home. Come home. She stared up at the sky, hoping that one of those messy stars would blink and grow, would land on her surface.

Time passed. Rapunzel grew. Mother lost hope for any other civilization, any other hope for humankind's destiny with hers.

Then the stars winked and blinked and a ship appeared on her skin.

She waited a day. A week. Moon after moon, the ship stood there in the desert. Silver, shining, waiting. It was as shiny as the stars it had come from, circular as a peapod.

Mother sent Rapunzel to explore it. If the people in the ship would not greet her daughter, then her daughter would greet them, and let them know they were all a part of Earth's family. Rapunzel would consummate with one of them, and they would create Earth's last great civilization. A collective of people to care for their true mother.

Rapunzel found the ship exactly where her mother had said it would be. Her skin had been calloused by the stinging of the sands, her eyes nearly blinded by the fierce winds. It was a simple pod that stood only a foot taller than her. She knocked on the tinted windows, tried to break them in with rocks and her fists.

It was so much simpler than that.

There was a door handle, like the ones she'd seen in the houses she explored as a girl. She turned it, and the door opened, leading her to the inside of the pod. It was cold metal with screens and little dials. There was a singular seat on the inside, and when she touched it, the material reminded her of silk and cotton fibers. So unbelievably soft, and so much kinder to her skin than anything Mother had given her. She sat down on it.

As long as humanity has existed, they have wanted community. Perhaps that was what prompted a human with a heart rockier than the planet they lived on to send a pod to Earth, to watch it descend onto the planet where he had grown up. Perhaps that was why he kept it under watch, why he kept waiting. Perhaps he had known there was someone down there worth waiting for.

Rapunzel had too many words in her head, too many thoughts in her heart. Earth had provided for her, yes, but there had been nothing for her there. How could you express the taste of the sky on your tongue when no one was there? How could her heartbeat alone sustain this vast, empty wasteland?

Mother had never asked her what she wanted. She had molded her like clay, but Rapunzel was not made of dirt and earth. She was a vine, green with new life, and you couldn't tell a vine which way to creep up the walls. The only thing you could do was watch it climb as high as it could, trying to brush one of the sun's rays.

The difference between vines and Rapunzel is that Rapunzel would touch the sun, and those plants would die trying.

Rapunzel had looked to the stars those past years, as humankind always had. She had prayed to the stars, begging them please, don't let me be lonely. She knew Mother had sent up flares, signals, anything to bring humanity back. She knew Mother wanted civilization like the ruins of the pyramids and those same, faceless houses. But what was a civilization without people in it?

Rapunzel had seeds in her pockets to bring to this new planet, wherever it was. She took fistfuls of red sand and sifted them onto the floor of the pod. She wanted to remember the life she had, the love Mother had given her,

She closed the door. The human in the skies saw, and Rapunzel was soaring through the air towards the stars she prayed to, in love with the sky and the adrenaline coursing through her veins. Mother was left childless and alone, free to grow and become everything that she couldn't be with humans there.

Perhaps that was the greatest gift of all.

Marauders vs Raiders

Yéeta Ku didn't dare sneeze when the suffocatingly sweet scent of Parde incense leaked into her nostrils the moment she threw open the door to her house. Even when one of the many scent bubbles that floated aimlessly across the main receiving room popped right in front of her face, she held her breath and pressed both her palm hard against her nose.

Ah, she thought as she waited for the irritation to subside, no earthquakes today!

"Ah San, Ah Rui." she called quietly. She let the bag she held in her other hand slip to the ground.

When its contents did not spill out as the bag slumped against the floor, Yéeta's inexistent smile bloomed to life. "I'm back from Merkat."

Yéeta raised an eyebrow at the silence that greeted her and figured that her aunt and her grandfather were now meditating.

It's been a long time since Ah San let go of his lif. A content grin touched her lips at the thought. "I'll not disturb them."

Yéeta took another quiet step inside and turned to shut the door, only for her to notice a hazy figure gracefully floating on the street across the house.

A prickle ran up her spine at the sight, and she had to consciously remind herself that ghosts were not allowed on Yéta One.

Her eyes watered the moment her gaze penetrated the swirling haze and landed on the woman that glared at her from across the wavy green and greener lines that formed the road.

Too bright! Yéeta blinked twice at the dense pink air that danced around her neighbor, barely able to keep her eyes from looking away from the blinding strands of starlight that floated off the woman's head and intertwined with the peach colored robed that garbed her pale skin.

The whole getup reeked of day-old matrimony.

"Yéeeetttaaaa." The woman dragged the name, a derisive smile slowly drawing against her lips as she slipped her hands into the large sleeves of her robe.

Yéeta let her hands fall to her side. She balled her fists and took in a breath to still the emotions that sent her heart pounding hard against her chest.

She sneezed.

The street shook and houses trembled.

The green and greener lines that wove the complex solidify-levator sigil that floated shuttles and people along the road shattered.

No head peeked out of their houses' windows as the road began the slow process of mending itself.

Miniature earthquakes were as common as the trouble Yéeta Ku's nose alone brought her and her neighbors had long given up on resolving every commotion that occurred in the once quiet neighborhood.

The expression of the woman across the street changed rapidly from shock to disdain, then metamorphized into something almost unrecognizable. It flickered about a dozen times amidst disgust and sympathy before settling on prideful.

Her smile widened a tad, wrinkling the corners of her eyes as she unhooked her hands and cupped them beneath her chin. "Don't tell me that at this age you still cannot control your lif."

"Càet, leave me be."

"Am I bothering you?" The woman giggled, a fan of pink aura shielding her face from view. "Well, I can't help it. Especially after someone announced that they had just arrived from Merkat. Isn't that the fictional Raider Starship?"

"Ye—" Yéeta coughed lightly when a gust of wind from inside the house wafted the Padre at her with full force. The so-called calming incense made the lining of her lips burn.

"I know that you are jealous of me, but there's no reason to bring Yéta One down." Càet tittered then walked off, her cheerful laugh resembling the gently chime of bells.

Yéeta did not smile. She kept her gaze on the floral patterns that were weaved into Càet's robe with her glittering white hair. The patterns that deemed her a wife.

Jealous, jealous, a squeaky voice whispered in Yéeta's ear, jealous that her husband was supposed to be yours.

Yéeta let go of her lif, imagining translucent tentacles extending from her forehead and feeling over every surface in sight.

Blood-red fruits rolled out of her shopping bag and sprawled on the floor behind her.

Without bothering to pick them up, Yéeta used her lif to fling them in the direction of the kitchen, before she herself stormed into her bedroom.

She did not see her grandfather or aunt on her way upstairs.

~

Yéeta stared at her grandfather quietly, her gaze solemn. She watched his hair rise and fall, up and and down motions that took his sky-blue hair soaring towards the ceiling then crashing to his shoulders.

Unlike the other times she saw Han Ku meditate, Yéeta did not admire the grey mixed in with her grandfather's hair to imitate clouds. She did not gaze at him in wonder and sigh twice more in admiration.

Instead, Yéeta dragged her gaze from her grandfather's pulsating hair and let it fall on the swords lying neatly across the table.

Her eyes burned. And not only because of the pungent odour that poured steadily out of the smoldering pot of Padre that sat just next to the weapons.

Yéeta knew that her aunt and grandfather had used the incense to hide the smell of steel from her, to keep her unknowing till the last moment.

They knew how much strong odours irritated her senses, so they didn't expect her to seek out its source.

Little did they know. . . Yéeta touched the tips of her fingers to the white cloth wrapped around her face then to the scarf she always wore. Its ends were wrapped tightly around her head to hide her hair.

She forced her gaze back to her grandfather.

He was looking at her now, his hair now the color of the night sky.

"Why?" she croaked, her eyes meeting his. "Why Ah San?"

"Ah Nee." For a moment, Han Ku looked pained. He took in a deep breath and extended his hands to the swords on the table.

He dragged his finger along each of their dim tips, causing faint sparks to run across the weapons.

Yéeta gasped when she felt her grandfather's lif thinly coat every steel blade, his dark hair shimmering with stars. "Ah San, you. . ."

Han smiled and withdrew his hands, folding them on his laps. "The Sun Sovereign's orders cannot be revoked."

"But you're old," Yéeta argued. "Your lif, it's dying. I can barely feel the strands. You can hardly control the swords now. . ."

"The Marauders are attacking, His Majesty's decree cannot be revoked. Every household must—"

"The Marauders are always attacking!" Yéeta shot to her feet. "I can't let you go to war in space, and against the Marauder's Nebulon of all star systems! You won't even get to be buried—"

"Yéeta!" Han shouted, then sighed. He gently patted the spot next to him. "You're already at marriageable age and you still act like a child."

Yéeta didn't say anything as she sat by her grandfather, her arms crossed as she glared at the floor.

"Yeta One needs all the able soldiers it can muster to survive."

"Yeta One," Yéeta winced at the name of their spaceship, then stared at her grandfather deeply. "It will survive without you."

"It is not that simple, Ah Ni." Gila Ku stepped into the room gracefully, links of armor draped over her arm and an aura of calm around her as her lif soared across the room and coiled around her niece in a tranquil manner. "Green and greener lines across the orbiter have been destroyed, so—"

"Ah Rui." Yéeta bowed her head slightly as she greeted her aunt. "You are in support of Ah San's decision?"

For a moment there was silence, before the woman let out a sigh, her obsidian hair darkening as she placed the armor in the table. "To disobey the Sovereign's decree is to seek death. . ."

Yéeta slowly got to her feet, her eyes downcast. "When will Ah San be leaving?"

"Tomorrow." Her aunt and grandfather answered together.

"I see." Yéeta said numbly and bowed twice to her family. "I'll be in my room," she moved to hug her grandfather, "don't wait for me. I won't be having dinner."

She hugged her aunt as she stumbled out of the room, and didn't look back.

I guess. . . this is goodbye. Yéeta had made up her mind. She wasn't about to let her grandfather green to his death.

~

Yéeta stared quietly at the short blade in her right hand and stifled a sob with her left. "Ah San, Ah Rui, forgive me."

Her trembling fingers shifted down the length of her hair, the gorgeous strands she had hidden since her parents' deaths and not seen since then.

It tickled her ankles and shined in the dark even when she wasn't channeling her lif through it.

Yéeta bowed deeply to the standing mirror in front of her, tears streaming down her cheeks. "Ah Mu, Ah Fu, forgive me. I brought you to your deaths."

Then the girl glared at her reflection. What she saw was not a gently soul with galaxies spun into her hair or a granddaughter ready to risk her life.

She saw a murderer.

Her hair that had ruined her family. It had caused the Sun Sovereign himself to bestow her the name Yeéta after the Yeta star and the orbiters that he ruled over.

Woven into each strand of Yéeta's hair was an accurate star map of the Sun Sovereign's territory. It showed accurate, real life depictions of Yeta's solar system and sourced Yéeta's lif through the power of uncountable stars.

And yet it was also because of this gift that the Sun Sovereign had accused Yéeta's parents of conspiring with the Marauders and had them executed.

Yéeta stumbled out of her room and walked slowly down the stairs, careful to be silent.

She stared at the front door for a moment before reaching out the handle and tugging it open.

"Life isn't fair." She raised the dagger and took a deep breath.

"Forgive me."

Yéeta walked onto the green and greener line road. "Zuzu, come out."

A bright blue light, the size of a firefly emerged from her shoulder.

What is it? the squeaky voice of the light laughed. Finally running away like a crybaby?

Yéeta ignored the zin's comment. "Denounce me as your master."

And why should I do that? You're too much fun to play with. Zuzu danced circles around Yéeta.

"I'm going to severe my lif."

There was silence.

You want to sneak into Merkat? It's glow dimmed to a flicker. You want to hide your identity. . . take your Ah San's place.

Yéeta only stared at the pulsating road, running her finger across the edge of the dagger. "I can get anywhere I want in Yeta, the stars are my domain. Males have their hair grow as they age, but the hair of women shorten with time. For my hair to be this long I have to be a man above one hundred. . . and that is impossible."

But women are allowed into the army! Zuzu cried frantically. You might kill yourself if you cut your hair.

"If His Majesty discovers that I'm alive, he won't spare my family."

Then you—

"You can't change my mind." Yéeta shut her eyes and imagined Merkat, the supposedly inexistent starship of the Raiders, knowing that the green and greener line road would sync with the coordinates of her hair.

"Zuzu, if you stay with me and I fail. . . our lives are linked by my lif, if it—"

Rest assured master, I have no intention of going down with you. But we both know nobody but you will take me as their pet.

Yéeta smiled, just as the road activated. "Good Zuzu."

~

six months later

Yéeta still felt a burn on her wrist, a stab in her heart and a twist in her lungs each time she took a breath.

When she tilted her head back she was just able to feel her hair brush the nape of her neck. It was so short, and she bore the pain for it.

It was a wonder that she hadn't died the moment she cut it, less surprising that her once luxurious hair had faded into a muddy brown and her lif could barely extend a metre.

"At least no more earthquakes." she laughed.

This greens, Zuzu protested dimly, you can barely control your lif, how can you fly a spaceship and control weapons at the same time.

"I'll manage," Yéeta pressed her fingers to her head in hopes of quelling the beast the fought in her skull. "The general asked for us."

For you! Zuzu sniffed and flew up to the ceiling. I'm the reason you're so popular among the Raiders. I'm the reason the general noticed your lif control skills!

"Okay, okay. It's all you. I'll get you a treat when I get back." Yéeta chuckled and shook her head, her short blade hanging off her waist as she leapt to her feet and left to the command centre.

"I wonder what mission I'm getting this time. . ." she thought to herself, suddenly feeling light and giddy. "The general wants to see me. . ."

Yéeta skipped down the halls while humming a tune.

~

This was not supposed to happen! Zuzu screamed in Yéeta's mind as a metre long sword pierced into the cockpit of the girl's fighter ship.

Why? Why? Why?! The zin cried, hovering over the sword now lodged in Yéeta's torso, pinning her body to her seat.

She couldn't get free.

"I had to save him. . ." Yéeta said quietly, her lips stained with blood as she stared blankly at the scene unfolding in front of her.

Spaceships zoomed in and out of deep space faster than her lif could track. Cold weapons were being controlled by the lif of numerous pilots, piercing and hacking away at both Raider and Marauder jets.

The stars glittered so brightly.

Yéeta coughed out a mouthful of blood then smiled, showing off her reddened teeth to her pet. "I have, no regrets."

"We are. . . close to fending off the invasion. We need, our general—"

The thought of the man she had spend months with warmed her heart, even with the absence of words between them and the utter lack of contact outside of the training grounds.

Somehow she couldn't just help herself. Not when a Marauder ship was sneaking behind the Raider's left flank with a sword floating by it, ready to be activated.

How could Yéeta have ignored the fact that the only man she had come to care about was about to die?

She suddenly laughed, startling the anxious Zuzu into stillness. "I didn't. . . I didn't even know when I moved."

Yéeta closed her eyes and smiled again. "But it, was worth it."

Yéeta! Zuzu cried as it's master went limp.

~

"It hurts."

"It hurts so much."

Yéeta's raspy voice filled the infirmary of Raider HQ.

She had yet to open her eyes, but for the first time in days, she was awake.

She felt a hand grab hers and went silent for a moment.

"Ge-neral?" She whispered, immediately recognizing the large callused palm.

"Why?" He asked back, his fingers tightening over her own. "You didn't need to risk your life. . ."

"A good soldier doesn't mind taking a sword for his general."

"But you are not a soldier, you are—"

"So you know." Yéeta made an effort to peel apart her eyelids so that she could catch his expression.

The first thing she noticed was how haggard the man had become. The second thing though, was her lif.

She gasped when General Kun Hé passed his fingers through her hair. It now reached her hips.

"I had my doubts." he told her, then fell silent. "There is no Yé Ku in the annals of the Ku family."

Yéeta swallowed back her dread. "Then why did you—"

"You have excellent lif control, and because of your bravery, we managed to defeat the Marauders' invasion once and for all."

Yéeta slowly sat up, looking at Kun carefully, without blinking. She took in the solar flares that erupted in his golden hair. "Is that all?"

"His Majesty has learnt of your identity and ordered for your execution." Kun slipped his hand out off hers.

"And you are to be my executioner?" she laughed bitterly in understanding and clasped her hands together. "Do it then, I don't see why you kept me in alive in the first place."

"The Sovereign's decree cannot be declined." The general stood up and placed his hand on the hilt of the sword.

Yéeta shut her eyes and bowed her head, a tear silently slipping down her right cheek. "You thought me not to fear death."

She waited in agonizing silence for the subtle sound of lif merging with steel.

"The Sovereign's orders can't be denied, so I don't know why I can't. . ." he said quietly. "I can't do this."

Yéeta's eyes shut open when she felt his hands cup her face.

"Yé Ku, be my wife." General Kun told her seriously. "Maybe its because you saved me, but I can't let you die."

"I can get His Majesty to rescind his order. Marry me."

"What?" Yéeta's eyes went wide. "Why must I marry you?"

Kun Hé pressed a thumb to her lips, his blue eyes shimmering. "Do you not want to?"

"I. . . I—" Yéeta gulped.

"By right I should have no hesitation to kill you," he sighed loudly. "So I need to understand why."

"And me marrying you is the best way to do that?"

Yéeta didn't let him answer, a grin splitting her face in two. "Since it's like that, I have no choice."

Kun Hé smiled back at her and leaned forward to press a chaste kiss against her lips.

Yéeta hummed in delight.

And just at that moment a firm knock sounded on the door to the infirmary. "His Majesty arrives!"

Spaceships & Glass Slippers

Clytemnestra had to be the ugliest planet in all the eight solar systems. Radiant red mist surrounded its surface, that was black as coal. Or at least that was what she imagined coal to look like. Humankind had drained Earth of it almost a millennium ago and gone looking for alternate resources elsewhere — starting the colonisation of space.

Rellaya sighed as she looked out of the large cockpit window, watching the dozens of other spaceships approach the planet before them. They were bright spots in the darkness of the void around them, painted colourfully, with hideous grimaces adorning their fronts, meant to repel the monsters that floated in the vast spaces between galaxies and fed off of human flesh.

Her blue ball gown brushed against her legs and her heels were already squishing her toes together uncomfortably. She should have gotten used to it by now, yet the silky skirts still felt foreign to her.

The wig she was wearing felt itchy against her scalp, the contacts were making her eyes dry, but she tried to ignore her discomfort while the captain called out to the crew to initiate their landing sequence.

One more job, she thought. One more ball and she'd finally leave behind her horrid stepmother and stepsisters and get a place of her own. After tonight she'd be free.

The pilots' greyish faces were glued to the screens in front of them, their fingers flying over the softly glowing controls as they typed in commands and adjusted engines. The Jack-O descended towards the planet slowly, upsetting and swirling up the fine fog of iron oxide that gathered in Clytemnestra's atmosphere and could be seen from space like a ghostly glow.

It took them a few minutes to reach the surface and land in one of the hangars owned by the royal family. Rellaya tapped her earpiece and the call was picked up immediately. Without waiting for a greeting, she spoke, "Landing complete, going in now."

"Copy that," came a voice from the other side of the line. A moment of silence passed. "Remember Rell, in and out. Good luck."

The call disconnected with a soft click and Rell lifted the hem of her dress to climb down the stairs. A mass of people greeted her as hundreds of other guests did the same, crowding in the hangar and pushing towards the entrance to the palace. She looked back over her shoulder at the Jack-O, that sat in its parking spot, waiting for her to return with their prize. Its bright orange colour reminded her of some fruit, or vegetable from Earth, that she only knew from pictures in history books.

***

The ballroom was just as pompous, yet airy as she remembered it. The ceiling was a huge glass dome that gave an unobscured view of the three moons that belonged to Clytemnestra. They were glowing like blood red jewels above the guests' heads.

Rell moved across the room, trying to stay away from the larger crowds and hoping she wouldn't run into her stepmother. Yet as she did so, she could feel the prickling of eyes on her neck. She pretended not to notice and continued her stroll when she sensed a movement to her right. She turned and a tall man dressed in a dark blue suit was standing next to her.

"Good evening, Miss," he said with a bow. "I don't believe we've been acquainted yet."

No, not any man but Adryan Wae-R'en himself, the prince and heir to Clytemnestra.

"I would certainly remember if it were so, your Highness," she replied and curtsied, giving him one of her rare smiles and doing her best to remain calm while her heart started to beat a little faster. "Isley Camran."

"Would you humour me with a dance, Miss Camran?" He held out his hand but Rellaya hesitated. She stared at it as Adryan looked back at her expectantly, his lips stretched into a slight smile. Rell avoided his gaze.

"Oh," she said. "I'm sorry, your Highness." She bit the inside of her cheek, chastising herself for her sudden nervousness. For a second, she felt like running, like abandoning everything then and there.

"Why, you must think me very ugly." He was still smiling, his eyes glinting and let his hand fall back at his side. "I suppose I must look just as alien to you as you used to look to me."

That's not it, Rell thought as she looked him over. He wasn't unattractive if one didn't mind the Cerulean looks. His body shape was close enough to that of a human with broad shoulders and toned arms. His skin was pale with that cool blueish undertone that came from the fact, that the Ceruleans' blood was indeed blue — hence their name. His hair was just as light, almost white but it was his eyes that she couldn't get used to. They were like quicksilver.

It wasn't like she was opposed to dancing. She had danced with a few other guests before, after all, she had to blend in with the crowd. But the thought of dancing with this man, had her heart leap strangely. She composed herself and gave him another modest smile.

"But why me, your Highness? Surely there are other ladies worth your attention gathered here tonight?"

"There sure might be," Adryan said. "But see, I noticed you at the last two balls but by the time I'd gathered up my courage to ask you, you were already gone. So my friend challenged me and I do not like losing to him. He's already smug enough as it is." He smiled at her again and Rell found that she wouldn't mind looking at his smile a little longer. "Though, if you insist, I will, of course, leave you be."

She blushed a little and this time, she didn't even need to act flustered. "If that's so, I suppose I can't let you down." She nodded and when he held out a hand once again she placed hers in his. His grip was firm and warm, not cool like she had expected, his light skin a stark contrast against the light brown of her own. Intricate golden tattoos were glittering across his wrist, slithering up his forearm and disappearing beneath his sleeve.

"We'll split the money he owes me," Adryan whispered near her ear as he led her over to where the other guests were dancing. His breath tickled the side of her neck and his words coaxed a chuckle from her lips. They swept in a wide circle across the dancefloor, Rell's skirts swishing through the air like a tail. She felt like the eyes of half the ballroom were fixed on her, or at least those of half the females in the room.

The prince didn't seem to notice as his silver eyes observed her. "Tell me about yourself. Where do you come from?"

"I was born and raised on Neptune. My parents made their money with hydrogen and hydro impulsion and I'm the heir to their business." It was only half a lie, close enough to the truth so she wouldn't trip over her words, he didn't need to know more than that.

"So you're here to find a suitable partner to form a union for life. That seems awfully familiar." Adryan's smile was still there but his gaze seemed more serious than before. The whole purpose of this festivity and the other balls before it, was for him to pick a bride after all.

"You got it all wrong," Rellaya smirked at him. "Actually, the only reason I came here for was to break into your treasure chamber, steal Cin'Lei's glass slipper and sell it for enough money so I could earn myself a nice little palace of my own."

The prince broke into a laugh that had the people in their vicinity turn their heads towards them and to her surprise, she couldn't help but think that she really liked the sound of this laugh.

***

An hour passed, then another and Rell realised she was enjoying herself. Twice she had picked up a drink for herself and the prince from the refreshment table. When the clock chimed, signalling the late hour, she was shocked to learn that she had completely forgotten the time and found Adryan to be, in fact, charming.

She fanned herself with her hand, noticing that her cheeks were, indeed slightly warm from all the dancing. A hand touched her arm and the prince leaned down towards her.

"I'm going to go catch some fresh air, want to join me?"

She nodded and together they squeezed through the crowd of dancing people. They moved swiftly towards the back of the room, up the staircase and to the part of the palace Rell knew wasn't used as frequently. They slipped through a sliding door and found themselves in an empty hallway, that was only lit by two blue glowing lines that ran along each of the walls. A strange quiet surrounded them now that they were away from the music and the crowd and Rell was almost afraid to break it.

"Where are we going?" she asked as she followed Adryan down the corridor. Her heart rate had picked up again and was now thumping against her ribcage.

He turned towards her, a smile on his lips. "I want to show you something." And grabbing her hand in his, he continued to lead her around the corner and into another identical hallway.

They walked for a few more minutes until they finally reached another door. Adryan swiped a palm over the touchpad on the wall next to it and it slid open. Rellaya found herself standing in a spacious room lit by the same lights she'd seen in the hallway before. Yet here, they covered the walls in glowing stripes, casting the space in soft pink and purple.

To her left, a glass staircase led to an upper floor that was shrouded in twilight. A massive window made up most of the wall on her right side, opening to a view of the palace and the city beyond it. Tiny lights twinkled in the red fog that rose up from the black mass that was the landscape of Clytemnestra. In the distance, jagged mountains rose from the ground, looming on the horizon like shadows. Two white couches and a tiny glass table were making up the centre of the room.

And then it hit her — they were in the prince's private quarters. Awed curiosity rose in her as she took in the room once again, noticing the little items scattered around. She wondered if the staircase led to his bedroom and the thought made her face feel even warmer than it had after the dancing.

In and out, she reminded herself. Just get what you came here for and leave.

"Here," said Adryan suddenly and stepped around her, further into the room and towards the staircase. She faintly registered that he'd taken off his suit jacket and was now wearing a white shirt that stretched across his shoulders. The rolled-up sleeves revealed his forearms and the tattoos on them. Golden ink swirled and moved beneath his skin, creating everchanging shapes. She was distracted for a moment and almost forgot that he meant to show her something.

Rellaya shook her head, hoping the action would clear her confused mind and moved up the stairs. A warm glow lit up the previously dark upper floor and the big glass case that awaited her when she reached the landing. Her eyes went wide and she didn't know what to say as she stepped nearer.

"You keep it in your bedroom?"

In the glass case sat, on a cushion of dark blue velvet, Cin'Lei's famous glass slipper.

Adryan leaned his shoulder against the side of the glass, facing her with a grin tugging at the corners of his lips. "Actually, my bedroom is over there." He jerked his head to the left. "Want to see it?" His strange silver eyes sparkled and Rell felt a blush creep back up her neck. But she ignored it and drew closer to the glass.

Every child in the eight solar systems knew the story of Cin'Lei and how, nearly 120 years ago, she had been the central figure in bringing down Osriel and freeing the world of his tyranny. And everyone knew the iconic glass shoes she'd been known to wear. The woman had been a heroine and her footwear became an intergalactic treasure after her death. One of them had been broken, which made the remaining slipper's worth dizzying.

"And you brought me here just so you could show off?" She raised an eyebrow at him but her gaze was drawn back to what was sitting behind the glass.

"I brought you here because I was hoping you'd let me kiss you."

She forgot what she'd been about to say. When she turned to face him again, he was beside her, looking at her intently. Rell bit her lip, aware of how his gaze trailed the movement. She felt her wit suddenly scattering and falling away, so much that she didn't know what to respond. Her eyes strayed back to the glass instead. She could feel Adryan studying her face in her reflection. "I wonder..."

She trailed off, unsure if she should finish the sentence but she didn't need to.

"You want to try it on, don't you?" He chuckled softly and shook his head but proceeded to tap the side of the glass. Rellaya noticed there was a tiny keypad etched into the pane. The case slid open.

He picked up the shoe and carefully held it between them. Rell couldn't move, just stare at his hands. She'd imagined this so many times, actually seeing it up close now felt unreal, like she was dreaming.

When he knelt down at her feet, she felt something rise inside of her, a feeling she couldn't grasp nor name. His hand was warm as it took hold of her calf and the other one slipped off her shoe. The glass was cold against her skin when her foot slid into the slipper but surprisingly, it felt oddly comfortable. She smiled to herself, looking down at her foot.

Adryan stood and straightened himself and as he did, he was suddenly towering over her. His quicksilver eyes looked down at her and she thought she might just be able to read the emotions swirling inside his iridescent pupils after all. He drew nearer and her heart beat so wildly she could hear the blood rushing in her ears.

"Did I tell you that you look beautiful, Islay?" He whispered, his breath brushing her cheek. And at that moment, she did feel beautiful.

She closed her eyes. He was so close now and drawing nearer still but she didn't dare move, afraid to close the distance, not ready to break the spell yet. She felt torn as her heart seemed to want to hammer straight through her ribcage, either from fear or excitement, she couldn't tell. She stood very still, waiting, the warmth of his body and the scent of him filling the space between them.

Somewhere in the distance, the clock chimed again, fireworks went off. The twelfth hour. Midnight. And just like that, the spell was broken.

Rell opened her eyes, peering up at the silver ones. But the prince swayed and she grabbed his shoulders before his legs gave in. He groaned softly as he sunk down to his knees.

"Easy now," she whispered. "It seems like you've had a little too much champagne, huh?"

"I—I only had two." His brows knit together in confusion, then he seemed to remember and his eyes widened. "Did you... poison me?" He tried to push her away but she was still holding him upright. He swayed again.

"It's just a little sleep potion," Rell said as she carefully eased him down to the floor. "You'll be fine in the morning, maybe have a little headache."

"What are you doing?" Adryan slurred, trying to stay awake but slowly losing the fight.

"I already told you," she replied as she rose back to her feet. She turned away with a last glance at him and started to walk towards the staircase. "I'm stealing Cin'Lei's slipper and buying myself a palace."

Cryosleeping Beauty

The solution fizzed bright red, hissing and spitting sparks out onto the pristine white lab counter like drops of blood on snow as Astrid carefully squeezed five milliliters of titanium out with her micropipet. The reaction was like a flash of light: bright for an instant and then calm again a second later as the solution returned to the original translucent pink color. Despite the nondescript appearance of her current mix, Astrid was satisfied, knowing that the one second reaction was just as long as she needed to produce the perfect serum--or at least it had been enough when tested on the adorable white rat sleeping by her bed. Perhaps one little test wouldn't have been sufficient were she still on Earth, but animals were scarce on the Andromeda, so this would have to be good enough.

Besides, it wasn't like she particularly cared about her next lab rat.

With steady hands, Astrid tipped the test tube into a syringe. She then placed the device in a clear protective bag, which she deposited into her large bag where it nestled among her other assortment of junk: hair ties, gloves, notepads, pens, hand sanitizer, and one other crucial syringe. Satisfied, she removed her white lab coat and goggles, zipped her bag and slung it over her shoulder, and exited the lab, using her unique thumbprint to lock it behind her. Out in the dim grey hallway, she hurried away towards the grander Central Plaza of the Andromeda, glancing at a clock along the way. The party had started ten minutes ago. She was late, but then again, her appearance wouldn't make a good impression on the gathering even if she were on time.

Astrid's mouth twisted as she thought of what she was to do. She had thought through all the possible outcomes, and knew that this was what had to be done. It would have been better, perhaps easing a bit of the stress from her burdened shoulders, had she been able to talk it over with at least one other scientist, but the poisonous lab experiment three years ago had made sure that would never be a possibility.

She knew that the people might hate her, especially the Captain and his wife, the First Mate. That would be far from ideal, cooped up on this ship with them for the rest of her life, but there was nothing to be done. Although it might make everyone avoid her even more than normal, she was far too precious to kill and everyone knew it.

After she reached the Central Plaza and turned off into one of the passenger hallways, Astrid was once again wowed by the breathtaking stars outside. No matter how many times she walked through these halls, she was sure she would never get used to the sight, the bright stars of glitter among a sea of blackness. And more than that--there was the unfathomable idea that she was part of the future looking into the past. The stars that shined so brightly might be from a time before humans had screwed up Earth beyond repair, might have burned out years ago but still continued to cast their legacy on their little ship.

After reaching the hallway, it was only a few more minutes before Astrid reached the golden gilded doors to the Ballroom. At the doors, she could hear slow, romantic music flowing from inside and realized that she was, as per usual late. It didn't matter. At least she could make more an entrance this way, even more than her usual unwanted attention. With a deep breath, she pushed both of the doors open. They were lighter than she expected and swung all the way open, slamming against the walls on either side with a bang. Immediately, all eyes in the room were on her.

"Well," said Astrid, fighting the urge to duck away from all the attention. "I suppose this is one way to make an entrance."

As she stood there looking out onto the sea of ostentatious party dresses probably passed down from Earthen generations, she noted wryly that her white lab coat--bright and similar to a skirt on the bottom--would fit in more than her everyday outfit that she wore now: tight black pants and a form fitting black turtleneck, her black hair pulled up into two tight space buns that, while ideal for keeping her hair out of her face in the lab, had also spawned rumors that she had horns.

Mustering up all her confidence, she began to walk into the room. The crowd parted instinctively, ducking away from the vision in black and making it easier for her to walk through the throngs of people. When she was around the center of the room, someone shut off the music so that the only sound was that of her steel toed boots--heavy duty to protect from lab accidents--clunking across the floor. She had a destination in mind, and the Captain and First Mate seemed to realize that and rise to the challenge, drawing themselves up fuller in their throne-like chairs. When she got to the front of the room, she gave a mocking sort of half courtesy.

When it appeared that nobody was planning on breaking the silence, Astrid decided to take initiative herself. "What a lovely party," she said mockingly. "I must say, I was rather distressed to learn I wasn't invited."

"You're not wanted here, Astrid." The Captain met her gaze with hardened eyes. "You're to stay in your quarters and out of everyone's way."

"Oh dear," said Astrid with a small laugh. "What an awkward situation. But shouldn't you know that you don't stop me from coming to anything?"

The Captain's face tightened, eyes narrowing, but Astrid glared defiantly back."Then you might learn to have some respect. I am your Captain, leader and driver of this ship, and you would do best to follow my command. Right now, you're making a scene on Aurora's special day. Anyone with basic human levels of decency should know not to do that."

"Yes, that's right," called a distinct, light voice that Astrid would recognize without even looking. Her songs were always playing around the ship in a mind-numbing sort of way you couldn't get away from. Where the voice was, the she demon was never far. Aurora floated into view in rose colored dress inlaid with so many gems--probably diamonds--that she looked could probably win a contest in being the best chandelier against the extravagant diamond chandeliers that hung on the ceiling. Her delicate hands were wrapped around the arm of a tall, scowling boy that Astrid recognized as her very publicly hailed boyfriend, Scorpius. He was always strutting around the ship as though certain he would be the next Captain just because a little fifteen year old girl had a fleeting crush on him.

"I'm sorry, but you really aren't welcome here, witch." Aurora's voice was so soft and melodic that you couldn't really help but to fall under her spell when she spoke: that was, of course, unless you listened to her cruel words. But nobody ever did; nobody ever looked past her otherworldly outward beauty.

"Nobody likes you; there's a reason you're never invited anywhere. You bring the stench of lowlife with you. Please, just stay with the rats where you belong."

Astrid rolled her eyes. She might have been furious as Aurora's insults if she hadn't heard them dozens of times before. The girl was as unoriginal as a five year old. Before the incident, three years ago when there were still other scientists, her mentor Leo had somewhat jokingly observed that Astrid might be flattered that Aurora thought the feats she accomplished through science and medicine were so like magic that she called her a witch. And she might have been, in a cynical sort of way, except that her limited interactions with the very superficial Aurora had made it very clear that the insult had much less to do with the incredible things Astrid accomplished and much more to do with the copious amounts of black she always wore.

She should never have hoped anything more, of course. Aurora's entire life revolved around her beauty and her privileged birth. At birth, she was gifted by the ship's two scientists a bit of genetic manipulation to ensure her prized, superior traits--her breathtaking beauty and melodious singing voice--just because her parents were the Captain and First Mate and wanted a doll of a daughter. And so she had never worked or studied or lifted a finger--probably had never even gotten dressed all by herself--for a single day in her life. She spent her days singing and embroidering and dancing and doing all sorts of useless things, enticing everyone who passed her wake, having the most ridiculously extravagant birthday party Astrid could ever dream up.

Meanwhile, Astrid had practically grown up in the lab, injecting herself with needles and serums when no one else would to test out new medicines and save humankind from going extinct. And on her sixteenth birthday, two years ago, she had spent the day alone alternating between curling up on her tiny cot and vomiting into a bucket every few minutes, side effects of a vaccine she was testing on herself.

"It just so happens," Astrid drawled, "that I came here to see you, Aurora. I hope I haven't missed the gift exchange yet?"

"I'm not sure I understand," said Aurora , her voice quivering slightly, betraying the smallest bit of her internal fear as she edged closer, using her boyfriend, Scorpius as a shield. Astrid matched her pace, stepping confidently closer to the dolled up girl. "It's not everyday you turn sixteen," Astrid said softly, taking three more steps until she was standing directly face to face with the girl. Her beautiful face, perfectly made up, looked more porcelain than human, especially with the large red rose tucked into her golden curls framing her face. She looked perfect in the moment, and Astrid hated her for it. "I thought I might give you a present."

Aurora looked a mixture of confused and scared as she stared down the girl, her rosebud mouth parting a little as she grasped around for a response. Her father answered for her.

"You've never given a gift a day in your life, Astrid," said the Captain. "I don't know what kind of plot you're messing around with, but I hope you realize there will be repercussions for your behavior. Take your gifts and get out of here."

"Oh, but it's only fair that I get to give my gift," Astrid said, reaching out and taking Aurora's hand in her own. The girl visibly flinched, but Astrid tightened her hold so she couldn't move away. "Leo and Orion gave you gifts that your pathetic little brain will never fathom the greatness of. So I thought it only fair that I get to give mine too."

And then, with a movement fast as light, she reached into her bag for the freshly prepared syringe. Pulling Aurora's arm towards her, Astrid pricked the point of the needle into her arm, plunging it deep into her flesh and squeezing down to inject the serum into the girl's vein. Aurora's eyes widened--with surprise or pain Astrid couldn't tell--and she stumbled backwards as Astrid pulled the device from her and threw it to the floor beside them. Aurora stumbled backwards, with Scorpius grabbing her and preventing her from falling. Astrid was vaguely aware that the entire room was staring at her, in fear probably, anger too, as she approached the girl, pressing two fingers to her neck to feel her slowing pulse. She pulled out the second syringe, ready to press this serum into her too, but the boy beside her was faster, knocking it away. Instead of her arm, it caught the girl's finger, where Astrid was quick to push it down. It wasn't ideal, but a pricked finger could still work.

"What have you done?" the Captain roared beside her. Astrid whipped her head up to see that he and his wife had rushed over and were now standing beside her, stony, fierce expressions on their faces.

"I've done her a favor you'll never comprehend," said Astrid, returning her gaze to Aurora, whose eyelids had fluttered shut and had gone completely limp against her suitor. Good. Then the first part had worked, at least. The first solution should have slowed down her heart, the second one, her brain, to a pace that was barely sustainable. She just needed to get her hooked up to the coffin like case filled with liquid nitrogen in the lab within a few hours to keep her alive, and monitor to make sure that all had gone as according to plan, especially with that deflected second injection. If not, Astrid had more she could inject into the girl, and was sure with a few scans of her brain she could monitor how much more she needed.

"Is she dead?" The shriek was obnoxiously high pitched and sharp coming from the Lady Captain as she hovered over her daughter. "She's not breathing!"

"Relax," drawled Astrid. "She's still breathing. Unfortunately. It's just at such a slow pace that human ears won't be able to detect it--only the machines I have in the lab."

"What have you done?" the Captain demanded again.

"I wish I could say that I killed her," Astrid deadpanned. "But unfortunately, her genetics wouldn't let me. This ship isn't going to dock at New Earth for a hundred more years, and we'll all be long dead by then. But the genetic enhancements that Leo and Orion gave Aurora at birth did more than just make her pretty; I've observed a startling change to her white blood cells that appear to make her, among other things, immune to any harmful virus that enters her body. Since there's no way of telling what kinds of diseases might attack us on our new planet, she really is essential for colonization. Yet with Leo and Orion dead, I don't know how to replicate it.

"Before Andromeda left Earth, the scientists there developed a technique to put people into cryosleep, and have always known that it might be essential to this trip. You or your answers--whoever first agreed to come aboard this ship--all signed off that it was a possibility at the scientists' discretion, for the better of all, although I wouldn't be surprised if you didn't take the time to decipher exactly what that entails.

"Anyways, I believe that Aurora's genetic code will be essential if we are to succeed. I have no way of knowing what will happen when she reproduces, especially with this ship being such a small population where detrimental genetic mutations are nearly certain to occur. The only logical option then, was to put her into cryosleep, slowing down her functions so that she's nearly frozen and ages much, much, more slowly. Her body and mind will still be sixteen in a hundred years when it's time to wake her up."

"You're taking away her life," breathed Scorpius, horror in his eyes.

"No I'm not," said Astrid rolling her eyes. "But I wouldn't expect you all to understand."

"Why now?" asked the First Mate, her voice quivering, eyes brimming with tears. "Why would you not tell us first? Why would you come disrupt her special day with such tragedy?"

"Oh, that," said Astrid, and she couldn't help the mocking tone that crept into her voice. "I must confess, I was a bit upset to learn that I wasn't invited. I did want to give my gift at her birthday celebration, you know! It just so happens to be that my gift was more like a... a finger prick, than a beauty product." And she had to admit, it was sweet to be in this role. She had loathed the girl for so long.

"You should know this is high treason to do this to a member of our esteemed family without consulting us first," the Captain hissed.

"Yes, I know," said Astrid. "But you know and I know that I'm the only scientist or doctor on this ship. You all rely on me because you've been too lazy or stupid to study yourselves. I'm the only one who knows how to wake her up, for one thing. So if you kill me... you kill her. And then you kill yourself and every single other person on the Andromeda in the likely occurrence of an illness or disease--anything that could spread and kill you all."

The Captain's teeth were clenched, but he said nothing. So Astrid only laughed as she turned and exited the room, reveling in the feeling. She would allow them all to collect themselves first, then come to collect the girl for her lab later.

Scorpius watched the scientist exit the room, looking more like an evil witch than ever. He had always disliked her and her mocking, scathing attitude, the way she seemed to take pleasure in making sure her treatments were as painful as possible, and lord over everyone how she had the power to keep everyone on the ship alive... or kill them all dead. Brushing a kiss onto Aurora's now ice cold forehead, he vowed that he would learn Astrid's ways, take out the witch, and save his true love.

Sister Mine

"Feet...c...cut...feet...c...cut...feet...c...cut..."

Sanneken bends down and picks up the shattered calf, brushing off dirt and shriveled rootlets. Deep, filthy cracks spiderweb across the purple plastic. Blaster holes. A blackened section where fire had blazed. She knows it's not the same as her stepsister, not quite. But it was part of her once, wasn't it?

She unwinds the recording, slides the silent piece of plastic into her pack and scans the landscape for a moment. Her fingers ghost across the handle of the shovel stuck in the ground at her side. A canyon of dry red rocks and sand stretches between her and the glittering palace in the distance.

The sky's fading to a green so dark it's almost black now that both suns are setting. Blue stars come out one by one, sparkling through the clouds. A bitter wind moans through the canyon.

This is no place for a broken young girl to die.

A crackle comes through the cobbled implant in her hard-of-hearing ear. "Keep an eye on those clouds."

"Yeah."

Wizard pauses. Her breathing through the link is the noisiest thing around Sanneken. Everything else has gone eerily silent in anticipation of the storm.

"You holdin' up all right?"

"Mm."

Two purple dots flicker on the holotracker, blinking out shaky coordinates. Sanneken glances at the canyon below her feet. The other pieces are down there somewhere. Familiar rage burns in her chest, ugly and sour.

"We can call it a night, Goldie."

"'M fine."

She ties the shovel onto her pack and starts down a couple of boulders that've fallen together. Could've rappelled, if she'd had the patience to bring her ropes and gear. If she'd had the time.

"Watch for the virava. They'll be coming out to hunt soon."

Sanneken grunts in reply. Down below she imagines she can already see their yellow eyes, winking softly in the twilight. She jumps from the boulders to the canyon floor. Her footsteps are quiet across the sand.

Cameras perch on the edges of the canyon like starving birds of prey. They turn in shaky fits and starts, worn down by the sand and storms. She ducks them easily.

"You're coming up to a fork," Wizard crackles in her ear. "You'll want to turn–"

The link goes static.

Panic and Sanneken have long been strangers to one another, but she is still on speaking terms with dread. She turns in all directions, squinting into the gloom, tilting her head to the right. There's no sound but the howling of the wind. Storm clouds float weightlessly across the stars.

Then a quiet clanking, the hum of smooth machinery. Sanneken shakes her head to herself. They only keep cams and virava down here, don't they? Wizard had said they did.

Wizard has been wrong before.

Sanneken isn't risking it. She's got nothing to fight a bot with and everything to lose. She dashes for the nearest boulder, crumbled against the canyon wall. There's a tiny crevice, big enough for a slim-boned child to barely squeeze through. She tosses her pack in through the crack and winces when the shovel blade sings loudly off the rock face.

The quiet clanking pauses.

Sanneken scrambles up the side of the rock. Her hands slip, frantically seeking a hold, but she launches herself over with her legs and tumbles through an opening at the top.

Hard rock glances off her arm, sandstone scrapes her cheek. She slams onto the dirt floor and sucks in a shaking breath. Too loud. Dust swirls through her nose. She clamps a hand over her mouth and feels her lungs scream.

The clanking is louder now, loud enough that Sanneken can hear the whine that lies beneath it. Gunmetal gleams in the gloaming through the crevice. It's coming right up to her hiding place.

The green lights on the top of the protocol bot wash over the boulder, flashing across the crack. Sanneken winces at the sudden bright glow but bites her tongue. Clacking noises. A deep metallic groan. The hum of machinery. She presses herself back against the rock, as far back as she can. Green light trickles over her boots, twinkling on the buckles.

She squeezes her eyes shut.

A thunderous rumble sounds in the bot's massive frame, and then it slowly turns away, clanking back down into the canyon. Sanneken waits until she can't hear it anymore before she slowly peels her hand from her mouth to exhale. No breath comes out.

"GOLDIE! DO! YOU! READ! ME! TURN ON YER DAMNED LINK!"

Wizard's voice is blistering. Sanneken curses and turns the volume nearly all the way down, her ear buzzing.

"Protocol bot."

"Sorry! Sorry! Thought you'd turned me off again, didn't know there was a bot in the area. Y'know, it don't show up at all on my radar."

"Maybe it's new."

"Forget the bot. I've got an idea. Try those newfangled goggles I slipped you."

"Wiz."

"Just give 'em a whirl! It's gettin' dark. You won't be able to see worth a damn out there soon."

Sanneken climbs out from behind the boulder first, throwing her pack over and following as quietly as she can. Her pulse is jumping all over the place, and she can still feel the hum of the protocol bot under her skin. Her fingers shake when she digs around in her stuff. The goggles are near the top.

She slips them on and watches the world go bright purple. "Now what?"

"Should be able to find a trail real easy. Go north towards the palace, stop when you come to a bent arch lookin' thing, and then head left."

With the goggles on, Sanneken can see everything in impressive detail up to ten feet away, but beyond that, no luck. Lucky she's always had a head for navigation.

She turns her implant volume up again as she trudges across the canyon. Wizard's strange goggles aren't good for anything but tracking. If the protocol bot is still around, she won't know until it's too late.

It's a long time walking through a bright purple landscape after that. Sanneken can feel a headache threatening. She's about to tell Wizard where she can stick her newfangled goggles when something pink catches her eye. A stain, on the edge of a downward slope.

She pulls the goggles up off of her left eye. Nothing. On the right eye, it's clear as day. A spattering trail of pink splotches snakes down into the dark.

Sanneken doesn't want to guess at what they are. Blood, guts, motor oil... Dornicka left her a path to follow. Like she'd told her to. Her eyes sting, and she snaps the goggles back in place.

The sky goes completely dark almost as soon as Sanneken finds the end of the trail. She drops to a crouch, hoping there are no working cams around. The first moon is barely rising, so it's hard to see much of anything, but her eyes catch the telltale glow of plastic, and her fingers brush across the curve of a hand.

There's a faint whine coming from the jagged purple stump. Sanneken lifts the arm from the dirt as carefully as she can and brings it to her ear.

"F...fingers...broke...f...fingers...broke...f...fingers...broke..."

She slips the arm gently into her pack, tucking the dangling fingers in before she snaps it shut. The recording coil goes in her pocket.

Faraway virava howls echo through the canyon. The pink starts again on the curve of a nearby boulder. She tugs up one half of the goggles to see if there's cams or something else to worry about, but it's so dark out she can't see a thing.

The trail winds down, down into the deeper part of the canyon. Rock towers loom over her, blocking out patches of starry sky. The wind whistles overhead. Every now and then there's a long stretch of purple without any pink stains at all, and Sanneken's heart squeezes in her chest until she finds the next one.

She's so intent on the trail that she nearly walks over the end of it when it abruptly stops. She drops to a crouch again, reaches out, and feels nothing. Thin air, even. Sanneken frowns.

"Found it yet?"

She pulls the goggles down around her neck and swears quietly. A deep pit yawns before her feet like an open mouth. She kicks a small rock off the edge. After a long moment there's a faint clack down in the darkness.

"I found it."

Now she really wishes she'd brought her rappelling gear. All she's got is a rope, which she ties around the closest rock arch and drops down slowly with, hand over hand, into the pit.

The air around her is so quiet it feels like the pit is holding its breath. Sanneken pauses on her descent, one hand and a leg tangled in the rope, and fishes in her coat pocket for her night vision goggles. She manages to pull them over one eye.

Long stalactites cluster around her like teeth. Rusted gears and wires line the walls, running down to the floor. She pushes the night vision goggles up, pulls Wiz's goggles on again. A thin pink line leads away into the dark.

Her lungs clench. She has to force breath into them, staggeringly loud in the silence. Dornicka was here, Dornicka fell from the lip of the canyon down down down–

She lands with a soft thud. Sand grits beneath her boots. There's a faint, clicking hum from beyond the clustered stalactites. Sanneken looks to the walls, but those gears haven't turned in a long time. Dread prickles at the back of her neck.

At her feet, the pink line has turned into a faded pink smear. She kicks at the smear, and smells a faint aroma of dried blood. Sick anger coils in her stomach. She pushes it back.

The trail of smeared blood lurches in a strange zig-zag across the pit floor. Sanneken experiments with holding the night vision goggles in front of Wizard's goggles, but it doesn't make a lick of difference. She settles for switching every now and then.

The electric hum fades as Sanneken moves deeper into the pit, which is quickly becoming a cave. The implant in her ear is nothing but fuzzy static. She smacks it a couple times.

Wizard's voice rasps through. "...good look at yer location, Goldie. Be careful...bot...big'un..."

"Do you read me?"

"Gold– no– careful–"

It cuts out again and won't work after that. Sanneken doesn't dare curse, glancing around the silent ceiling of the cave, dripping with stalactites. Logically no bot could have made it down here, but she's no fool.

Stalagmites sprout from the cave floor the further Sanneken follows Dornicka's fading trail. She almost crunches the last piece under her boot, since the pink keeps going on and on and...Sanneken's fists clench, but she forces herself down to a squat.

A pair of spheres brush against her fingertips, and the recording is so faint she can't hear it at all beyond a rasping whine. She palms both eyes, cranks her implant up to full volume, and holds them right next to her ear.

"S...anneken...S...anneken...S...anneken...S...ave meee..."

Her implant cuts out on the last part of the word, and the ensuing static drives pain straight to Sanneken's temple. Wizard was right.

A telltale clanking sound echoes from her left. She scoops up poor Dornicka's eyes, clambers in among the stalagmites, and a massive mecha foot crunches down on the place she was just crouching in.

All the air leaves Sanneken's body in a hoarse gasp, but the whirring of the bot covers it. A bot? No, it's much too big to be a bot, but what else could it be? Its massive metal head brushes the ceiling, knocking off stalactites here and there, and its lights sweep the cave in a gigantic ray of eyewatering green. The electric whine drills down into the base of her head. Her heart beats a triple tattoo so fiercely it feels like it's set to leap out of her ribcage.

She crouches back against the cave wall when the bot's light swings over to her hiding spot. Her elbow cracks off the top of a thin stalagmite. The sound is like a blaster shot in the cave.

Sanneken's mouth goes dry. The massive protocol bot turns slowly to her, as loud as thunder. She drops to the floor, pressing herself as flat as she can, curling around the stalagmites like a patch of moss. A massive blade on the bot's arm slices six feet deep into the rock where her body had been.

It waits for a moment, clicking and whirring. Sweat runs stinging past Sanneken's eye. She forces her breath to hold. Its blade scrapes out of the cave wall at a snail's pace. The green light flashes over Sanneken's prone form, and for a moment she can't breathe, or move, or think. The bot slowly pivots and thunders on down into the next cavern.

Her heart won't stop racing after that. A trickle of air finds its way down her throat. Chunks of crumbled rock dust her shoulders and hair from the bot's blade. Her implant crackles in a burst of Wizard-sounding static. Sanneken closes her eyes in relief.

"Goldie! You there? Sweet Medusa, I've got this monster of a bot on my map- a damned jailer! I didn't know they still made 'em!"

"How'd it get down here?" Sanneken whispers. Too loud. She turns down the volume on her implant.

"The dungeon lets out into this cave of yours, kid. You found the back way in!"

"Good."

"Didja get the last piece yet?"

Sanneken uncurls her hand, revealing the two twinkling plastic eyes. Her palm shakes, and she hurriedly closes it again. If those clatter onto the cave floor the bot will kill her for sure. "Yeah."

"All right. Follow me!"

It takes her longer than it should to find the small metal. door at the opposite end, but every click and clatter sends Sanneken to the side of the cave, watching. The bot is so massive her implant is always crackling with static, but she makes it to the dungeon stair.

The lock hasn't been opened in years. Sanneken snaps the chain in half and shoulders her way in. A hinge breaks in a scream of rust and disuse, and she races up the mildewed stairs before the bot's sword arm can impale her on the door. From here she can hear laughter floating from the cell block.

"Always the wicked stepmother!" someone shrieks, and the laughter starts up again in full force.

She finds her mother in the smallest cell, curled in a shivering pile, and pulls the hinges off the cell door. Her mother startles awake. Her face is hollowed out with grief.

"Hey," Sanneken says, and staggers back at her mother's fierce embrace.

"We can't let him have Zlata," her mother whispers, eyes big and angry, like Sanneken has to be convinced. "We can't let him have her too."

"We won't," says Sanneken, and draws a hasty summoning circle on the floor. Wizard appears in a hazy cloud of static and hot air, all her white hair standing on end.

"You look lovely, Bea," she says to Sanneken's mother, who smiles.

"Thank you, sweet."

It's quick work to get into the palace. Guard bots are stupider than cams, and the dungeons aren't more than glorified cellars. The corridors are empty, polished to a blinding silver sheen. Blue lights flicker like candles, casting the three of them in a strange glow.

More bots cluster in front of the banquet hall doors, brandishing blasters and stun spears. As soon as Sanneken gets her hands on one of their spears, she makes hash of the rest and stabs the control panel on the wall, hidden by a decorative curl of metal.

The intertwining locks snake all the way up the doors, unlocking joint by joint by joint until they swing open on silent hinges.

Bright golden light and music pour out from the banquet hall. A vast white table stretches the width of the room, covered with food and surrounded by guests.

At the center of the table sits the king and his ravishing young bride. He offers her a forkful or tender meat and she jerks her head away, tears streaming down her cheeks. A long chain stretches out from underneath the tablecloth.

Sanneken leans over to the herald. "Introduce me as Dornicka's sister."

The herald does so, and the king's head snaps up. Guard bots surge forward, but he holds up a hand.

"You enter my court uninvited."

"I have a message for you," says Sanneken. "The truth."

"Truth is rarer than any treasure," the king replies. His left eye glows blood red. "What is your message?"

Sanneken produces the three recordings, coiled into Wizard's hands, and begins pulling them through her fingers like thread. A young woman's scream splits through the air and the wedding guests startle. Zlata's face crumples.

Then comes a shaky, sobbing voice– Dornicka's voice, taut with pain and fear. "First he took my feet, my feet. He cut them with his knife. He broke my fingers and he cut my arms. He cut my throat. He drank my blood and ate my body. Next my eyes. Oh, sister mine,

I know he will take my eyes. I know he will take my eyes. I know he will take my–"

Zlata jumps to her feet. "Sanneken, save me!" she screams. The king pulls her back down to his side.

"Guards!" he barks, but as soon as they circle round the banquet table, electricity leaps from Wizard's silver fingers, and the bots go down one by one. The banquet erupts into a panic, guests trampling one another in their hurry to escape, screaming and shoving. The king rises slowly from his table with Zlata's chain in his hand.

"You are a brave one. I'll give you that," he says. Zlata stumbles weeping behind him. "I did not know there were three of you. I'll give you that. But you cannot hope to triumph, girl. I take whoever I want for whatever purpose I choose. I have seven secret names written on the foundations of the world. I can pluck the lightning out of that spear, and the heart out from your chest. I can live and live and never die. What power can you possibly turn against me?"

Sanneken smiles.

***

Beneath the battlements, the virava tear him to pieces.

Even Space Hags Gotta Eat

Colony 2474 was three days from starvation. It made Greta furious. She'd told them repeatedly, they needed to send scout ships to ask for aid but no, they pinned all their hopes on a failing agricultural experiment and look where it got them. Down to nothing but fried dried rations that made cardboard an appealing substitute. The dregs, bottom of the barrel. She swore if she flicked her stomach it pinged like a hollow drum.

"You knew they wouldn't listen. They're scientists. We should have gone ahead without their permission." That little nugget of wisdom came from her brother, Hank.

Greta snorted. "Like I could get your ass moving any faster?" Hank reminded her of an overgrown cat, lazy, full of rampant disdain, and willing to claw your face off if you got between him and his precious naps.

He glared at her. "All you had to do was mention food." True. The man thought with his stomach. It was amazing he was so lean, though she long suspected he contracted some sort of space parasite he refused to acknowledge, like an interplanetary tapeworm.

"Ew," she shuddered at the mental image. She spun the pilot's seat to give the navigational chair a nudge with her foot.

"Hey, make sure you leave a flare trail before you settle for a nap."

"Yeah, yeah," Hank yawned. He punched a button. "Breadcrumbs deployed. Wake me up when you find something." He sank back in the chair, his feet up on the control panel miraculously between buttons. Out in five minutes, snoring softly, and left Greta alone with her thoughts. She was incredulous.

How did he do that? Just curl up and dump all the anxiety in her lap? Technically 'finding something' was his job as navigator but it wasn't worth the yelling to wake him up.

Find something. The proverbial needle in a haystack, except this haystack was infinite and the needles could be anywhere. Greta sighed and hit the distress beacon. If they had a scrap of luck, they might find a functioning way station. At this point she'd take a passing freighter or mercenary ship. The colony gave them enough funds to purchase supplies. Money wasn't the the issue.

"Idiots," she murmured. Coming out here wasn't even her idea. Her father and step-mother dragged the two of them halfway across the galaxy into the unknown nearly ten years ago, when Hank and Greta were two young to live on their own. Their parents were agricultural scientists, who know damn their attempt to cultivate the colonized land was failing but refused to give up until the problem hit critical mass. Hank called them glorified space farmers for a reason. Three days, if they managed some creative rationing, they could push it out to a week. It was impossible window of time. People were going to starve before they got back. There was absolutely no way--

The scanners pinged, picking up a broad bandwidth signal.

"No way." There it was, sharp and clear, like a lighthouse beacon in a storm. A rush of excitement flooded her system. She snapped a kick at the back of Hank's chair that dislodged him to the floor. "Wake up! We got a hit!"

Hank went from scowl to wide eyed in two seconds. "Seriously?"

"Take a look." She leaned back as he examined the readings.

"Too good to be true," he said.

"Oh come, a fully operational space station this far out? We'd be insane not to at least check it out. This could save everyone we know."

Hank rolled his shoulders. "Doesn't feel right."

"Screw you and your feelings. I'm starving and I'm sick of freeze dried protein packs."He scowled at her. "You think I'm not? What the hell is a fully operational station doing this far out? This quadrant is a galactic shit hole."

"We shipped out over a decade ago. Any number of things could have happened since then."

"Including bad things."

"What does that even mean?"

"That we shouldn't trust the first thing we see," said Hank. He crossed his arms over his chest. "But I will concede a closer look is necessary."

"How reasonable of you," Greta sneered.

They settled in their respective corners. Greta's eyes were fixed on the monitor when she tensed at Hank's softly murmured 'uh oh.'

"What now?"

"Uh I seem to have deployed the wrong flares."

Greta ground her teeth. The ship was equipped with two types of flares. A long lasting pulse flare they called a bread crumb and a flash bang, which had a short life span and snuffed out after an impressive array of fireworks. No breadcrumbs meant the trip home would take even longer, possibly get lost. She wanted to throttle him. "That is a rookie mistake."

The insult equated to about the same thing in Hank's eyes. "You're right. I screwed up." Greta focused on the read out in front of her. He admitted he screwed up, no point in yelling at him now. The minutes ground on, until their ship pulled close enough to catch a glimpse of the station through the view screen. Greta flipped it on and stared. From here, the station was lit up like Christmas morning, a brilliant clusters of lights among the stars. Her mouth started watering at the prospect of her first non ration meal in ages.

"Something wrong," said Hank over her shoulder.

"Would you quit being a cynical bastard?" After his screw up with the flares, he should be grateful their luck finally swung in the right direction. "We are docking and checking it out."

Greta sent out the standard greeting signal and waited.

Hank pointed. "I don't see many ships. Do you?"

She would strangle him before the day was out. There were at least half a dozen ships nestled at the docking ports on the station's entry ring. It was a low number of ships for a thriving station but any number of factors could account for that. "It's a new station, they might not have a great deal of traffic yet." She spoke through her teeth and if Hank had a lick of sense he would back off now.

Time dragged without a response.

"Maybe everyone is busy with the three ships they have docked," Hank muttered. Greta spun, ready to lay into him when the station's return signal lit up her screen. Finally, something going right. Sort of. It was an automated message of welcome and instruction to dock at the nearest port of convenience. Contact with an actual person would be better, Greta could inform them of their situation, but she wasn't going to look a gift station in the docking port.

She maneuvered them in closer, using the manual controls to steer them to one of the empty docks. Up close, the station didn't look so appealing. There were some obvious signs of outer wear and tear, borderline shabby, that wedged the first sliver of doubt in her thoughts. No, no, they needed to at least try this place. Shabby or not, the docking clamps locked onto their ship and a green light pulsed over the outer door to inform them the oxygen seal was intact. Least they would be able to enter the station without containment suits.

For all his surly attitude, Hank beat her to the door, rocking on his heels. "You coming or not?"

Idiot. She held her breath as the door hissed open. Sterile white light spilled into the shadowy recesses of their ship, near blinding after so many hours with just the light from their consoles. Greta shaded her eyes and squinted through the light. A figure waited from within, their hands clasped in formal greeting. A real person at last, the tension drained out of her spine.

Greta elbowed Hank aside and stepped forward as the figure spoke.

"Greetings and welcome to the Cottage. I will be your guide. You may call me Sumi."The Cottage? An odd name for a space station. From Greta's memory, cottages tended to be small isolated buildings in the middle of nowhere. Well, technically the Cottage fit latter part of the description to a tee.

Sumi possessed delicate features, from her pointed chin to the high ridges of her cheekbones. She studied them with eyes so dark they appeared black, with a polite smile on her pale lips. She gestured out to the main body of the station. "If you would come this way, I will show you to the main concourse."

Hank closed up the ship behind them as they followed Sumi. The exterior of the station held obvious signs of disrepair, but the interior was pristine. Walls in white and chrome rose in a cylindrical column, the floors a stack of rings around a crystalline core; the solidified carbon based fuel that served as a power source for space stations without a planetary power source. Greta's gaze was drawn to it repeatedly, mesmerized by the mirror sheen. Sumi walked before them with a sway of her hips as she lead them to the main concourse. They entered a lift to ascend. Hank leaned close the murmur in Greta's ear.

"It seems awfully empty."

"Don't be rude," said Greta. "We haven't even seen the main concourse yet."The lift slid open. They exited and froze. Sumi kept walking until she seemed to realize they were no longer behind her.

"This way please."

If they didn't follow they'd lose her completely, because the main concourse was swarming with Sumi clones. Identical features, identical uniforms. Hundreds of them clogged the concourse, chatting and laughing in a hum of feminine voices. Greta and Hank exchanged a look. What was going on here?

"Come along. We have a meal waiting for you," said their Sumi.

A small battle took place in Hank's expression. She knew how he felt. The vibe was weird, the horde of Sumi clones downright bizarre. Hank's stomach growled. He surged after Sumi with his hands fisted at his sides. Greta bit the inside of her cheek and followed. The crowd parted from them as if they were a barge on water. A heavenly smell wafted through the air. Greta's mouth pooled with saliva. Hank moaned.

"It smells like apple pie," Hank glanced at her, eyes wide and filled with longing. They hadn't so much as smelled an apple since they left Earth for the colony. He might have a better memory about them than she did, because all she could smell was roasting meat, like a Sunday Roast. She swallowed to keep from drooling and followed Sumi with renewed interest.

Clone, android, whatever their guide was, it didn't matter, not as she lead them into the alcove of a stall to a feast.

Platters of food filled the staggered shelves, various roasted meat, vegetables, candied fruits, pies, some recognizable, some not but all of it steaming and gleaming in the bright white light. At the center of the room, behind a waist high counter, stood another Sumi, except this one was obviously different, older. She possessed the same delicate features, but there was an edge to her smile and an expectant gleam in her eyes that might have given Greta greater pause if the scent of food wasn't short circuiting her brain.

"Welcome to the Cottage, wear travelers," said the woman with a bow of her head.

"Please, eat your fill and we shall discuss what business brought you here." Her words were cultured, with an accent Greta couldn't place. Hank didn't need any more of an invitation. He snagged a plate from a waiting stack and heaped his plate full of goodies. Greta slowly followed suit.

Something was nagging her about this set up. Through the yawning ache in her belly, there was an alarm bell trying to make itself heard. She loaded up a small selection of morsels to silence it and took a seat beside her brother at the counter.

The woman behind the counter watched them with a steady unreadable gaze. Creepy. Greta frowned at looked at Hank. He was completely focused on his meal as he shoveled food in mouth. Greta rolled her eyes. No help there. She cautiously nibbled on a piece of meat. The savory piece melted on her tongue. It was the best thing she ever tasted.

She managed to bite back a moan to save her pride but quickly brought the next piece to her mouth. The woman behind the counter smiled with closed lips.

After several mouthfuls, the edge of hunger eased enough for Greta to talk. "We didn't expect to find such a well stocked station this far out."

"We are a newer installation," said the woman behind the counter. "The station itself is older, one that tried and failed to establish itself this far out. You should have seen it when me and my girls took over." Her nose crinkled with distaste. "Little more than a dump. But as you can see, with a bit of polish and hard work, we've made it shine." She spread her arms to indicate the station at large.

Greta swallowed her mouthful and glanced up. "It's very impressive. Do you get many visitors?"

She wondered where the other occupants of the docked ships were. If she had the choice, she'd never leave this part of the ship.

Maybe they were shopping in one of the many outlets along the main concourse.

"Sadly, the pickings are slim this far out, but it's safer for us here," said the woman.

Greta paused with the food halfway to her mouth. "Why safer?"

Hank continued to shovel food into his mouth without pause. The woman made a dismissive gesture with her hand.

"Oh you know, prejudice and all. But out here, it is safe for me and my daughters to conduct ourselves as we wish."

That got him. Hank choked on his food. "All these women are your daughters?" His words squeaked at the end.

The older woman grinned, revealing a mouthful of sharp triangular teeth. The food dropped from Greta's fingers. Hank swallowed hard next to her.

"We should get going," Hank said faintly.

Greta glanced around. Her eyes caught on a pile of fabric beneath one of the food stands, a shredded pile of fabric she recognized as one of the Universal uniforms of station residents. The clothing was heavily stained with rust colored patches. Greta shifted in her seat, the urge to bolt strangling her. This station wasn't abandoned, it was taken over. The residents likely met the same fate as the occupants of those docked ships.

"No, no, stay, eat your fill. I insist," said the woman. Greta looked at her. Her face looked thinner, sharper, there was something wrong with her. Was she taller than before. She placed a hand over her chest. Her fingers were far too long and sharp at the ends. "I know what it's like to be hungry. It's a terrible feeling. Please, enjoy your meal so that we may enjoy ours."

"Time to go." Greta jumped up and spun for the door, Hank a second behind her. The siblings stopped short.

The entire horde of Sumis blocked the entrance, staring at the pair with identical expressions on their flawless faces. Hunger.

"I'm sorry. I'm sure you understand."

The siblings turned at her voice. Hank gasped. She towered over them, a spindly creature, long claws like sickles clicking together.

Her features were stretched and gaunt, a hollow hunger that shone through her black eyes. “I am a provider, and my children are hungry.”

Eyes of the Beholders

"The young lass 'twas so quiet, she could barely hold a lie, 'twas the elder's cruel riot, who removed her sweet eye."

A soft tone slithered through the evening air, gliding across a ruby red lipped canvas. Faint beams of light invaded the violet colorized-glass that surrounded the darkened room, saturating into the sagging wrinkles of the white washed cotton.

"Lids coated by gold, lashes laced with ore, the elder thought 'twill be a trifle sold, he would send it to the shore."

Each stroke of the gold soaked bristles slid down the portrait, while equally golden eyes narrowed upon a brown blemish that had appeared on the nose.

"The young woman mourned for the eye that she'd had host, but the vicar chastised her to no end," The brush came to a halt against the throat's crisp coated skin. "Tis wiser to rebuke the old and the lost, than to revel in the evil and the misfortune it will send. "

"Isla."

Wood scraped against wood as a thin pair of hands placed the tool back inside its oak whittled case.

"Isla, are you able to hear me, dearie?"

They dressed the painting in a crêpe colored veil before swiveling around to rip down another that sat by their side.

"I know you can hear me, I see the quirking of your lips."

With her face half hidden in the shadows, the young woman shrugged, the wisps of her cream kissed curls plaited down her back.

"Perhaps it is in my best interests if I were to ignore you, Méméře."

"I wait here for fifteen cycles of the lunar-sentient phase for you to tell me you don't feel like addressing my presence. Cast me back into the whirling abyss if you must, but spare me the attentions of that...man."

A short chuckle squirmed up Isla's throat, prying her lips open just enough to catch her Méméře's glance.

"You know how much I despise him! And I refuse to allow you to confine me to the same amount of space as him and his... hobbies."

Water poured leisurely over Isla's pallet, as did her smile over her face.

"You know how much Pépére appreciates your visits."

"Of course he does! I'm the only one in this wretched place, safe for himself and a few others."

Isla raised an eyebrow, placing the circular tray into a nearby bin. "You know that it is my conscience you are co-inhabiting, and I'm not sure you are doing what's best for it."

The short scoff echoed across the ridges and valleys within Isla's brain, followed by what she could only presume was the rolling of eyes and muttering under her breath.

"It would do you good to listen to it for once, sweetie."

"I do listen, Mémére. It's avoiding the voices that I find difficulty with."

Exiting the room, Isla walked down the metal lined hallway that led to the main sector of her home. Steam rose from a large bundle of cogs and wires that snored with each beat of its oil driven heart in the center of the room.

Isla scooped up a bucket from next to the slumbering beast, before standing atop a foot stool to pour the contents down it's burning throat.

"Just a few more days, Mi Ange," she murmured, patting the metal affectionately.

She leaned her forehead against its side, taking a deep breath as that familiar throbbing in her fingers began.

"Isla! You ungrateful cow! Where are you?"

Her lips tightened as she stared up a skeletal spiral staircase. "What is it, Veda?"

"You forgot to clean the exterior of the carrier! How do you expect to earn your place when all my mother has done for you has been out of the kindness of her heart?"

"Is she speaking of Satan again, dearie?" Mémére guffawed, her voice farther off than it had been a few moments before.

A smirk dashed across Isla's face again. "I'm not quite sure, Veda."

"Of course you aren't," Veda spat, descending the stairs with her nose tilted upwards. "It would have served my mother better if she had left your cursed mother to rot in that well."

"Has she ever seen a looking glass before?" Mémére's voice grew fainter, and it was as if Isla could see the illuminated pathway between their two worlds fading. "I must go for now, dearie. I shall return soon... do be careful."

"I'll try, Mémére," Isla whispered. A cool sweep of sadness caressed her cheek as Veda approached, chocolate colored eyes smothered in waves of disgust.

"Crying. How pathetic."

Veda shouldered past Isla, approaching a large panel that had been built into the ship's mainframe.

Isla's head whipped to the side with the weight of a flashing silver suit and a larger silver helmet that Veda threw at her from the controls.

"Get on with it, before we all expire from self induced asphyxiation,"she sneered, pressing her hand into the power console, which was soon followed by a short, high pitched whistle piercing the air.

That familiar tug against her shoulders drew Isla further into the dark void that lay beyond the carrier's forcefields. Pulling the material over her body, she snapped the suit into place while the helmet secured itself with a hiss of pressurized air.

Isla tore a long cord from the wall near the black opening, attaching it to the back of her suit. She peeked over the edge of the drop off before stepping back a few paces. Veda smirked at her from behind the panel, waving her away with her hands.

"Not scared, are we, Isla?"

Not giving her step-sister an opportunity to respond, Isla broke into a sprint, running across the platform and plunging into the welcoming arms of the black abyss beneath her.

Despite being tucked away inside the suit, Isla could feel her hair being whipped at by the ever present winds, tearing at her clothes and her skin as she tumbled through time.

She knew needed to find the handle attached to the other side of the ship, otherwise she had no idea whether or not she would be able to pull herself back from the void.

Her stepmother had warned her of the dangers in casting oneself into the void, but the dark territories that served as home to many aboriginal cultures since the Soleil explosions had long been thought to contain something more ancient than the lunar settlers themselves.

The darkness was a means of travel, had been as long as Isla could remember, however, something was wrong this time. Her hand flew through the shadows, searching for any grip on the reality she was meant to be in, yet all she could feel was a sweet, chilled breeze nipping at her fingertips.

"You need to reach out now," a voice whispered.

Isla tensed while her fingers stretched. "Who said that?"

"Does that really matter? As far as I can see, you have found yourself in quite a great deal of error."

"How are you able to see anything?"

"Reach."

As Isla threw her arm farther out into the darkness, she screamed as cool fingers wrapped around her wrist and pulled her to the right into a deeper darkness.

"Where are you taking me?" Isla screamed, scratching at her wrist, only to discover it was her skin she was fighting against.

"Where did you go?"

"Nowhere," the voice murmured, and the grasp on Isla's wrist vanished as her feet connected with the ground and she fell to her knees.

Gasping, she pried her eyes open and fell onto her back with a scream.

Green. That's all her eyes could seem to take in as she yanked her helmet off of her head.

Earth. Was that what surrounded her? Clean, breathable air that she inhaled? She didn't know how it was possible.

She propped herself back up and slowly removed her suit, holding her hand out to see if anything would grab her again, but she felt nothing.

"You're quite a curious one, aren't you?"

With a shriek, Isla swung her body around, only to come face to face with a elderly woman in a white shawl. The woman smiled, her wrinkles bunching around the corners of her eyes while a mouth full of terrifying teeth caused Isla to raise her guard.

"I hope I didn't startle you, dear. I do have the habit of it."

Isla took a step back, smiling hesitantly. "Only a little. I wasn't expecting you."

"Not many do," the elderly woman chuckled, patting Isla on the cheek, "I was walking along and felt that I needed to ask for a favor from you."

"How did you know I was here?"

The woman winked, "Intuition you would call it. And where would you think we are, dear?"

Isla's eyes travelled around the pair of them, coming across grass, a small mass of fur, which startled her to see running across the ground, and strange wood-structured plants standing hundreds of feet off the ground.

Her skin had begun to warm, while a strange, transient light faded in and out behind large, frost covered fluff in the sky.

She felt her brows furrow as she turned back to the old woman. "I'm not sure. I've never seen anything like it in my lifetime."

"It's not Earth, merely a settlement in the Finire quadrant. I could hear you thinking it, now come along."

The old woman's grip on her arm was tight as she guided her through the grassy field. The voices in Isla's mind had once again gone silent, and it was clear she wasn't going to be receiving any helpful advice.

"How do you know what I was thinking," Isla said, walking slower, "if I might ask?"

A spark lit up the woman's eyes. "You may ask, and you were practically shouting it at me, dear."

Isla shook her head, and slowed her pace further as they approached a petite wooden cabin, shrouded in feathery foliage and white and blue bundles.

Opening the door, the old woman smiled and directed Isla towards the kitchen table. Much like the outside of the house, the inside of the abode was just as warm and fragile-looking. Trinkets lined the walls as far as Isla could see, while a sweet smell wafted over from the stove.

The older woman carried over two stone cups, steam rising from their rims as she set one down in front of Isla and took her seat with a sigh. While she drank, Isla sniffed the cup and looked back up to her, "Excuse me for all the questions, but you must admit this situation is odd. I'm not meant to be here. I'm supposed to be cleaning a carrier—. I don't even know your name."

"Mother Holle, dear." The woman smiled again, nodding towards the untouched cup. "And you should have no fear, I didn't poisoned your drink. It would be a bit rude on the first visit, wouldn't you think? Would scare off the neighbors."

Isla laughed, voice cracking when she took a small sip. "I'm curious as to why you invited me in the first place, is all. What is it you have to ask me?"

"The very thing I asked of your mother!" Mother Holle exclaimed, as if the answer should have been clear to begin with.

A shiver ran down Isla's spine and she tugged the sleeves on her arms down further. "How did you know my mother?"

"Did she never mention me?" Mother Holle shook her head, and walked over to one of her many shelves. "I would say I'm offended, but your mother was such a sweetheart I feel it would be an insult to her memory."

"You know then." Isla found herself stating, the metal against her skin beginning to burn again.

"Of course, dear. Now, to my proposition, before those pesky relatives of yours cloud up your brain waves."

Isla's head jerked up, eyes blown wide. "How did you--"

Mother Holle chuckled. "Some things are best left to themselves, but as I am sure you have noticed by now, you are stranded in this place for the time being and have no means to take care of yourself. Your mother fell, quite literally, into a similar situation like this."

"When she fell into the well," Isla murmured. Her mother had told her the stories before she had died, and the marks on her skin were the truth to her tale.

"Precisely."

Smiling, Mother Holle returned to the table with a small paper package in her hands. "All that I will ask of you is to help me. I am quite old in age, and these brittle bones don't agree with me like they used to. In exchange for your help, I will provide safe travels for you to return to your home, and I will also give you this gift, as a token of my gratitude."

"Help with...?"

"Oh simple things. Aiding me in cooking meals, cleaning around the house, and making the beds. However, I would ask that you shake out the covers in such a way that the feathers would fall in every different direction, for scenic purposes."

Isla nodded slowly as a voice called out to her from the darkness. "Isla? Isla, you must be able to hear me, it's much lighter in here than usual."

"Not now, Mémére," she whispered, smiling at Mother Holle.

"Don't ignore me, child. Who is it that you are speaking to?"

Stretching her hand out, Mother Holle smiled back. "Do we have an agreement?"

"Isla," Mémére shouted, "What are you--"

"Yes." Isla smiled. "We have an agreement."

Other voices rose in protest in Isla's mind, but she drew a dark veil across them all as Mother Holle clapped her hands together.

"Splendid! Let's get started then."

~~~~~~~~~~~~~~~~

Within the few weeks that followed, or what Isla believed them to be, she worked hard alongside Mother Holle as they tidied up the house.

Cobwebs collected and dust bunnies gathered, Isla worked both day and night for her caretaker, with not so much as a peep of complaint. And above all, she made sure to fluff the bed to perfection.

As she tucked in the covers one day, her sleeve accidentally slid up to her elbow, and much to the delight of Mother Holle, displayed the opaquely designed lines against her skin.

"No need to worry, dear," Mother Holle laughed. "I gave your mother the very same blessing when she worked for me."
~~~~~~~~~~~~~~~~

"Blessing?"

Mother Holle raised an eyebrow. "Have you never tried to see what the decadently golden lines themselves can do?"

"Never."

"I suggest you give it a whirl the next time you're around your stepsister," she cackled, her yellowed teeth shining as she worked .

Isla frowned. "How do you know of my sister?"

Mother Holle winked before heading back down the hall towards the kitchen, while Isla ran a finger down the thin golden scars that had been engrained in her skin since birth.

Ignoring further question, Isla followed suit and returned to the kitchen for dinner.

The next morning, however, a faint voice lifted the thick velvet curtain that she had laid over her mind weeks before.

"It's time to go home, Isla."

Shivering, a muscle in Isla's jaw twitched. "No."

"Don't be so prickly, Isladora."

"Don't call me that."

"I quite agree with her, dear." Mother Holle called out, hobbling over from a small section of flowers with clumps of dirt in her hand.

"I don't understand how you can hear her either!"

Taking ahold of Isla's arm, Mother Holle began to guide her back down the lonely pathway. Birds chirped in the distance as they came to a stop in front of an old gnarled trunk, something that she had quickly learned to be called a tree.

"It is about time that you returned home to your family, Isla."

The old woman placed a hand over Isla's heart, immediately causing the younger woman to draw back.

"What if I don't wish to go?"

She chuckled, holding her hand out. "Does the snowflake every wish to fall? Or the apple to ripen and leave its sweet branches? Life wasn't meant to be simple or comfortable, dear, and now it is time to face it with your head held high."

A tear raced down Isla's cheek. "But what am I to do?"

"Be brave."

Mother Holle placed her hand back on Isla, murmuring a few words, and then placing the silver laced package into the young woman's hands.

"Your mother would have wanted you to have it," she murmured, stepping back with each word. "Now go."

Isla ripped through the wrapping of the box to peer inside, just as her vision began to fade, her feet lifted from the ground and the voices of her Mémére and others began to flood her mind.

"Isla! For the love of all that is—!"

"You promised you would never—!"

"The carrier still isn't clean—!"

But they all paled in comparison as Isla scooped up a gold-encrusted circular machine from within.

Wiping away at its top, she turned it over a few times, gasping aloud as she clicked a button hidden in its side and a compartment slid open.

"...lids coated by gold..."

Her fingertips smoothed over the heated machine, her mouth falling open.

"...lashes laced with ore..."

Purple irises sprung from the purring gears, mechanical clicks ticking against Isla's palms.

"...he would send it to the shore..."

"Welcome, Isla Galia." It chattered, freezing the air in Isla's lungs.

"W-what is it you want?" Isla murmured, stumbling back into the darkness.

All was silent as the whirring of the eye came to a halt on Isla's rigid figure, clicking and groaning with each movement. Hissing as a paper shot out from its side, it illuminated the outer space around them as it whispered.

"I wish to show you the possibilities."

The Rattenfänger

"Okay. That should be the last one, Cap'n," Rattenfänger said and waved the writhing sack in Captain Wilheim's face. The middle-aged man jerked back at the claws smacking against the fabric and the frantic squealing coming from inside.

Space rats were disgusting little vermin. Much like the rats Earth got yet with six legs, a long tentacle tail for grabbing and holding their food as they munched and rows of tiny yet sharp needle point fangs.And the screech they produced was a cross between an Earth fox and an Earth Owl. It was piercing enough to make anyone nearby cover their eyes and clench their teeth in a cringe.

Rattenfänger's lips curved into a sharp-tooth grin and amusement twinkled in his large, black eyes at Captain Wilheim's open disgust at the alien in the bag. Those round eyes were unblinking, mainly because he didn't have eyelids, as he tossed the sack into the cart with the other bagged up space rats.

"And you'll take them to be burnt?" Captain Wilheim asked.

The grin disappeared from the alien exterminator's orange-tinted face. "Absolutely not. They'll go back to the planet you snatched them from. A bit of respect is needed here, Cap'n."

"We did not snatch them. They came aboard the Hamelin when we landed."

"Curious little things," Rattenfänger cooed, smiling down at the wriggling sacks. "They go wherever they smell food. Keen senses, you see. They can smell from miles away. Compliments to your chef for making some fine meals. No, sir, I'll take them back into me little ship and set them free in their natural habitat. They didn't do no wrong."

Captain Wilheim sniffed loudly, turning up his nose at Rattenfänger's plan. "Not exactly our agreement."

"Better than the torture you want to put them through. And that was our agreement. You asked me to get rid of the space rats. I did exactly that, I did."

"By singing?"

Rattenfänger hooked his hands behind his back, straightening with his chin raised in a wide smile. "Me species are the best exterminators in the Saxony Galaxy. Our voices hypnotise our chosen target and they follow. Pain-free, torture-free and gets the job done like that." He snapped his long, bony fingers. "No need for unnecessary killing, Cap'n. Now, I'll take me payment and be off with ya. Thirty Deutsche Marks, please."

Captain Wilheim looked the orange hand that was extended out to him, palm upright and ready to take the money owed to him.

"Funny..." Captain Wilheim said, rubbing his chin. "Funny how we've had trouble catching these space rats and yet all you need to do is waltz in here, sing and they suddenly coming out of their little hidey-holes."

Rattenfänger's hand dropped and those bottomless pits for eyes narrowed. "Just what are ya suggesting there, Cap'n? You radioed me, remember?"

"Thirty is an awfully high price to charge for a simple yodelling. I'm afraid I don't exactly trust your skills, Rattenfänger. There shall be no payment."

Rattenfänger was silent for a few seconds, gaze fixed on Captain Wilheim and for a brief moment, the Captain thought that forked tongue that kept darting out to lick his lips was a sign that he was about to eaten alive. But the alien exterminator slowly smiled and the cheerful glint was back in his eyes.

"I see, Cap'n. Well, I'm a no-contract exterminator so I gots nothing in writing to argue against ya."

"No, you don't."

"My fault I suppose, we're a generous species."

"Indeed. Perhaps it might be best to require contracts."

"I'll be off now, shall I?"

Captain Wilheim forced a tight-lipped smile. "Of course. Have a safe journey."

Rattenfänger pushed the cart out of the engine room, smile still present on his face. He was alone in wandering the labyrinth of corridors, following the signs to the departure lounge where he pulled his visitor pass off his neck and dangled in front of the receptionist.

"I'll be handing this in, darling," he said before he suddenly cried out and dived for a bag. "Oi! I can see that little claw popping out. Don't ya be escaping now! Darling, would ya get me another sack before this little blighter comes running out."

The receptionist squealed and dove into the back room at his request and he reached over, stretching his long arm to grab another visitor pass from the desk. The receptionist hurried back in, waving a sack frantically at the exterminator with the squeals continuing.

"Thanks, m'dear. I'll just pop it over this troublesome rat. I've caught all of them so your little infestation problem is all sorted. Have a good one!"

He smiled and waved at the cringing receptionist as he walked through the double automatic doors and towards his space pod.

The visitor pass was safely hidden away in his pocket.

~

The clocks on the spaceship Hamelin read midnight. In the middle of the Saxony Galaxy's solar system, the Hamelin was still in space, hovering over the twin Earth planet Erde. The moon that orbited, dubbed Mond, had now disappeared to the other side of the planet signalling night on the side the spaceship was stationed. At least, that was how the colonists ten years ago decided to time aboard the ship.

Captain Wilheim looked down on the planet Erde. Towards the other planets in this newly discovered solar system, all named after German mythological creatures. There were colonists down on Erde now, trekking around this new planet, and creating new communities on the discovered land. Aliens from the neighbouring planets were all chipping in to help this new human race settle. Another five years and the ship could go down to begin the official move once the planet was thoroughly checked and ready for settlement.

Hopefully, this planet isn't infested with as many space rats like Knecht Ruprecht was, Captain Wilheim thought and shuddered thinking of those small but noisy, pesky aliens. Disgusting vermin.

He was forced out of his thoughts when a loud siren howled through the ship. The alarm lights flashed red in his office and there was yelling and crying outside in the corridors. Captain Wilheim jumped up from his chair and keyed himself out, almost running straight into the arms of a panicked woman.

"My little girl! My little girl!" she wailed, clutching onto the sleeves of his uniform.

"Now calm yourself, woman. What's happened?"

Second-in-command Grimm dashed up, saluting the Captain once despite the wide panic in his eyes.

"Sir, it's the children. The children have gone."

"What do you mean? Where have they gone?"

"No-one knows, sir. They sneaked out of their beds and disappeared. All of them."

Captain Wilheim was about to bark orders when the speakers in the walls crackled and a feathery singing voice could be heard. It echoed, beautifully melodic and almost full of sorrow. The Captain felt his skin turn to ice at the familiar singing voice.

Rattenfänger.

"He can't just lure the children out of the departure lounge! We'll go there and get them all back."

"He's not there, that's the first place we checked."

"He has no authorisation to go anywhere else."

Grimm stiffened, eyes averting to the side and Captain Wilheim gritted his teeth. "He has no authorisation to go anywhere else. Correct?"

After a moments pause, Grimm replied in a hushed voice. "There's a visitor pass missing."

"Who checked him out then?"

"His badge was checked back out. He must have got hold of another one."

Captain Wilheim marched down the corridor. "Send men to every loading bay. Every holding cell. We need to find those children!"

"Sir?" An officer waved the ship's tablet map in the Captain's face. "Someone's got into Loading Bay one."

It was a rushed stampede of security guards as they raced down the corridor towards Loading Bay one. As they drew nearer, they heard the giggling of children. The delighted squeals and the pitter patter of small footsteps. Captain Wilheim pressed his hands to the glass of Loading Bay one and peered in, crying out.

The children were dancing and running around in the bay, playing near the gates. Above the gate there was a countdown, red numbers getting smaller and smaller...That signalled when the gates were about to open.

And the number was on four when Captain Wilheim saw it.

Fists banged against the glass, screaming at Rattenfänger who sat in his small pod. The alien pest exterminator waved at them with a sharp-tooth grin creeping up on his face. He flicked a button above him and leaned forward in his pod.

"Next time, Cap'n, we pay for the services we ask for."

There was a blaring alarm, shrieking over and over again as Loading Bay One was lit was red flashes. The gates pried open with a long creak and the children's squeals were cut off, replaced with piercing screeches of terror as they were sucked out. Pulled into the black void of space where their screams were cut short. Their arms and legs flapped and kicked for all but three seconds before they became still. Lifeless, they floated.Rattenfänger followed suit, reversing out into space and sped away from the ship; through the sea of dead children.

The gates closed and Captain Wilheim stared in silence at the now empty Loading Bay One.

Pyxis

Bowers watches the bulk of the Hesiod crest into view over the curvature of the asteroid to which his smaller spaceship clings. His fingers itch to touch the ship's flight sticks and maneuver it closer to their prize. The Hesiod is only a delta-class ship, but as a mining transport vessel, could hold untold wealth inside. Commercial grade explosives, or better yet, extracted ore. Both would bring a premium price at the black market.

"Two days, Gull. No directional thrust. She's just floating there, aimlessly."

"A wise man once said, 'Not all who wander are lost'. It's not abandoned." Gull replies in his frog-like voice.

"Three life signatures, and one has been stationary the entire time. Could be someone in cryo. We'll be long gone before they remember where they are. That leaves two others. Two of them, two of us. I like those odds." Bowers caresses the space ship's joystick.

"I'm almost finished unlocking remote access. Unless you'd like to get in your suit, float on over there and knock on the door?" Gull opens his mouth, showing off a black-gummed sneer.

The pilot mulls it over for a moment. "It would give me some time away from your geriatric stink," he says, "but we'll play it safe for now. On your watch, did you see the one leave its room?"

"No."

"So, one wanders the ship freely while the other stays confined. A prisoner, maybe?"

Gull taps at a keyboard, his eyes never leaving the monitor. "Could be Pandorum. Some boot gets the space-jeebies and has to be lock-and-keyed lest he drives 'em into the nearest supermass."

"I'm gonna drive us into a black hole if you don't finish your da-"

"Got it." Gull's screen lights up green as he hammers a final key.

Bowers slaps the dash of the ship and refrains from pulling the flight sticks back full throttle. Instead, he flips switches overhead to put them into stealth before using short bursts to propel them forward in a parabolic path.

Nobody says a word as the men cruise the ten kilometers to the Hesiod. Bowers pulls up broadside to the airlock.

Gull sets back to clacking at his computer and the bridge extends from the carrier to the scavenger's ship. The hacker smiles, "Rapunzel, Rapunzel, let down your hair."

The ship sways as the bridge makes contact, then settles as it engages its locks. The two men stop at a small armory chest before exiting. Bowers moves for a firearm.

"Not the hard light," Gull croaks, "We don't know the interior. Could make for ricochet madness. Bring the Slug-Plug."

Bowers grabs a 12-gauge snub-nose revolver and loads the chamber with four cartridges. He makes a quizzical face at Gull, who picks up a pair of daggers.

"What? I'm old school."

The men cross the bridge to the Hesiod's crew entrance. The metal creaks against the vacuum of the void outside as Gull opens the mechanical door. There is a rush of air when the pressures stabilize between the ships.

They enter a long, well-lit corridor that spans a lazy arc. "Cargo hold first," Bowers says, "We'll set up an ambush there for the roamer."

Gull nods in approval. They turn left towards the rear of the ship, passing no doors, but a thick floor-to-ceiling plexiglass creates a window into the bowels of the ship. Inside are crates of living supplies, with open boxes methodically moved to one side in a series of makeshift aisles.

"There's no place to lie in wait," Bowers says, the disappointment dripping in his voice, "We'll have to find a way into the hold."

"It's probably safeguarded," Gull chimes in, "If it's digital, I can hack it. But if it's biometric, we may have to find the sleeper and take his hand. Or his eyes, depending on the lock."

"And if it's voice?"

Gull clicks his tongue. "Well I hope you plan to be very persuasive with the remaining crew, Captain."

Bowers points to his shipmate's blades. "I think I'll leave the persuasive tactics up to you."

Nearing the end of the curve, both men slow to a stop, staring at the miracle behind the plexiglass wall.

"Holy nova..." Bowers whispers, taking in the sight. It is a small tree, seven to eight foot in height, with leaves a hue of green that no one has witnessed naturally in centuries. Small fruit bloom from the branches, but are undistinguishable, as neither Bowers nor Gull have seen anything like it before.

"I was in Atsim on Uranus last I saw one of these." Gull mutters, his voice dry and scratchy. "Just a boy, right before we left the system. They called it the Copse, and they had dozens of 'em. It was twenty years on a hard labor moon if they caught you trying to take trimmings."

Bowers' lips curl up into a smile. "It may not be explosives, but consider me blown away." Both men laugh at the cheesy joke. It comes out with a hint of mania as they consider the financial repercussions.

The chuckles die out when a young woman steps out from behind the nearest row of crates. She moves cautiously, glancing about as if to ensure that the scavengers are the only ones there. One eye is wide and blue like sintered cobalt. Her other eye is hidden behind a cascade of ash blonde locks that trail almost to the floor. Both features are a stark contrast to her caramel skin and full, umber lips.

Her hands hold a small wooden box, her fingers nervously trace the ornate inlays and crevices. "You must help me," she says, "I have to get home."

Gull scoffs. "Slow down Princess, we don't have to do a thing. Maybe we will though. How do you get in there?"

"She put me here. Trapped me in this flying tower away from my home." The woman speaks so fast her sentences come out like a single word.

"Flying tower, I see," Gull shoots Bowers a mocking look, "But how do we get in there? With you? And where, pray tell is home?" He presses his hands against the plexiglass, searching for a seam.

"It's a door, here." She lets one hand go of the box and places it on the other side of the window. Gull moves his hand over hers and a holographic keypad glows from the clear material. He takes a small digital device from one of his pockets and scans the keypad, then runs a program to decrypt the code.

"Earth," the woman says, "I'm from Earth."

Again, Gull looks over to Bowers, but he seems to be transfixed by the box the girl holds. "Nobody's from Earth anymore, and there hasn't been for centuries. Only thing it's good for is battery storage and strip mining."

"What's in the box?" Bowers interrupts.She hesitates before answering, "It's just a toy. Something from home."

The first digit blinks on Gull's decoder, with five more lines still flashing through iterations. "She's messing with you, boy. She's not from Earth and neither is that trinket."

"Then where did that come from?" Bowers points to the tree in the distance.

The woman slowly steps away from the plexiglass. "She's coming."

The lights in the ship blink off, plunging them all into darkness.

Gull holds the decoder up, the LEDs giving off a few inches of visibility. There is a pop and buzz from a filament igniting. A short distance away, a glowing line of red appears. Gull draws one of his blades.

The thin red line quickly advances in an upward slash, Gull screams out as his decoder and dagger hit the floor. The hacker drops alongside them, sobbing. Still glowing, the filament turns to Bowers, who unloads two barrels directly into the center of it. For almost a full second, air escapes and cabin pressure drops when the slug tears through the hull. The sucking sound immediately wanes as the shell's plug expands, filling the hole with a rapid-hardening epoxy.

Emergency measures trigger, bathing the ship in soft light and harsh sounds.

An older woman slumps backward, held standing by a plume of quick-weld which connects her to the floor via the slug's trajectory. She wears a nametag that reads 'Lt. Grimm', which is quickly covered by the epoxy as it bubbles and hardens from a grapefruit-sized cavity in her chest.

Grimm wheezes something, but Bowers can't hear it over the alarms or Gull's continuous whimpering. He leans in close to her mouth, trying to discern her words before the arteries pump the epoxy to her brain.

"Don't... don't...." Is all the woman exhales, then her arms hang limply by her sides.

The alarms go off when the ship automatically re-pressurizes, and the lights stay on. Bowers turns to examine Gull, whose arms are gone, cauterized just below the elbow. The severed limbs on the floor still grip his dagger, as well as the decoder with the six digits to unlock the keypad.

"Jesus, Gull. What am I supposed to do with this mess? You can't even help us get home now."

Gull stops sniveling when Bowers' words dawn on him. "I'm only useless for a bit, Captain! We'll take the money we make from the tree... I'll get cybered up! It'll be even better then before!"

Bowers raises an eyebrow.

"My half of the money from the tree?" Gull counters.

"Problem is, friend, I want the girl too. She's not as valuable as the tree, but think how much a flesh-peddler would shell out for a real Earth girl. And there's just not enough room on the skiv for all four of us."

"I don't take up much room anymore..." Gull holds up his stumps and gives a desperate chuckle.

Rather than answer, Bowers reads the decoder and punches the numbers into the keypad. A seam appears in the plexiglass and a section slides away to create an aperture. Bowers hefts the gun towards the woman. "The box. Toss it here."

She steps back and holds the trinket to her side, like a small child trying to hide something from a stern parent. Bowers lowers the twelve-gauge level with Gull's head.

"No! Cap-"

The piece roars, bringing with it the déjà vu of momentary suction, lights, and alarms. A gray circular plug replaces the center of Gull's face, making him eerily featureless.

"That was my friend," Bowers says, retraining the gun on the woman, "Imagine what I'll do to you. The box, now."

She takes a step forward and Bowers thumbs the hammer back.

"I said... toss it."

She gently throws the box through the opening and Bowers catches it one-handed.

His fingers find a cleft, which shifts and separates the lid. A tendril of green slinks out, gingerly wrapping itself around Bowers' finger before budding a leaf.

"Another tree?" Bowers asks.

The vine continues crawling from the box and up Bowers' arm, its caress turning into a strong grip.

"What's going on? Make it stop!"

Bowers tries to turn his pistol to the box, but the plant shoots to his gun hand, controlling it with a vice-like clutch. He grunts as the vine expands, longer and thicker, snaking its way up his neck and engulfing his head. The more he struggles, the tighter it squeezes.His cries are stifled when the vine sprouts thorns. They dig into his hands, making him drop the pistol. They pierce Bowers' eyes. Behind the thick foliage, the intense pain is the only way he knows he is blinded.

He can hear the woman speaking from outside his verdant tomb.

"You are a Captain, you must know how to fly... and I'm in need of a ride home. Looks like you will be saving me after all, my Prince."

The thorns burrow into his muscles, setting fires as they settle next to nerves. Bowers mumbles a choked prayer for death.

Instead, the vines move inside his legs, and he shambles toward the Hesiod's cockpit.

The Glass Foot

Rosa didn't believe in many things. She didn't believe in fate, she didn't believe in destiny, and she definitely didn't believe in karma. But what she did believe in was a good strong drink, and oh boy did she need one now. Not that she'd ever be able to get one.

"You want me to do what?"

The prince of the Aesar Galaxy shifted in the seat in front of her, the yellow plastic creaking and contrasting badly with his tailored black suit and overcoat. His long fingers tapped on her dirt-strewn desk, but he avoided looking her in the eye. Rosa's tail twitched with irritation and loathing, the red band around it flashing softly with her annoyed heartbeats.

"I want you to find my fiancée."

"You want me to find your fiancée," Rosa drawled. "Your fiancée who, if the rumors are true, is also a murderous Plithia princess who spews fire and has four glass feet."

"Well, three glass feet now. She shed one." He pointed at said glass foot, now perched prettily on Rosa's desk like some sort of extravagant paperweight. Was one less foot supposed to be an improvement that ignored the whole murderous fire-breathing thing?

Not that Rosa was one to talk or judge at this point, but still.

It was amazing to think that the prince across from her was her friend growing up and later her boyfriend for what would be an ill-fated attempt at romance. Turned out, he just really wasn't her type, although she certainly was his. But nothing went to plan. At least not hers.

Rosa glared at the prince.

"Rosa, you're good at this kind of stuff!"

"No I'm not. Just because I caught the rogue lupine doesn't mean I'm suddenly qualified to take down a plithian. Also, what are you even doing trying to marry a plithian? They eat their spouses, Kane."

Kane shook his head, the silver tattoos on the side of his face glittering in the dim overhead light.

"She's truly a beautiful being, Rosa. Truly. Fascinating, really. She'll be perfect."

"Well yeah, that's the point. Beauty is how Plithians attract their prey. Her prey being you."

"I'm not her prey, if anything she's mine." Rosa hid a grimace as he leered. She changed the subject.

"How did you lose her? We are on a space outpost in the middle of nowhere. There isn't that far for her to go."

Which was very true. The Devian outpost was small. A space colony floating on the outskirts of Aesar, only people with no home, no family, and nowhere else to go ended up here. Like Rosa, the abandoned, black-tailed mechanic.

This was the place for the outcasts of Aesar as well as one of the fringe science facilities. There truly was no inbetween.

"I don't know. She said she needed to feed. One minute she was there and the next she wasn't." He put a hand through his dark blue, almost black, hair. Rosa pursed her lips.

"Oh for- and you just let her? Kane, Plithians eat other beings. That's what feed means. You know, for the crown prince of a galaxy, you sure are far too arrogant and irresponsible for anyone's good."

Least of all hers, and maybe the princess's too, if Rosa's suspicions were correct. She really hoped they weren't.

"I'm not irresponsible! In fact, I'm perfectly responsible. That's why I'm marrying Elana. At least for a bit. It's diplomacy, really. And you know my top priority will always be the collection, anyway."

Dread started to creep into Rosa's mind. Oh no.

"The collection-"

A loud blare sounded as the intercom system sprung to life.

"Rosa Haverfield to hangar six. Rosa Haverfield to hangar six." Rosa groaned, getting to her feet with a huff. Maybe he'd leave her be now. Brushing down her cargo pants and straightening her red jacket, her tail flicking, she walked to the door of her office, Kane on her heels.

"Wait, where are you going?" He trotted along to keep up with her, his long coat swishing around his knees.

"Hangar six, obviously." Rosa ignored the stares as they passed a group of female engineers, each of them eyeing up Kane. One of them sneered at Rosa. Kane didn't notice.

"I thought you were going to help me," Kane said, his voice sharp. He managed to get ahead of her, moving to stand in front, but Rosa swerved out of the way, maintaining her quick clip.

"I help you only as long as it's convenient to me, and right now, it's not convenient to me. That's always been our agreement, Kane. So stop following me and go find your fire-breathing wife."

"Fiancée. And I think you need to remember who you're talking to, Rosa." The words were a warning. One that Rose chose not to heed.

"Fine, fire-breathing fiancée. Whatever." Rosa quickened her pace, but Kane still kept up, staying level with her to the best of his ability. They passed loading docks and labs, workstations and tool shops, but he kept up the pace.

"Why are you still following me?"

"I need your-"

"Help, yes, got it. But can you please just not? The quicker I get to hangar six, the quicker I can help you. And honestly, you really shouldn't be tagging along."

"Why not? I am the prince. If anything, you should be following me and doing what I say, not the other way around. That is your job."

The more time she spent with Kane, the more Rosa remembered why their friendship ended.

"No, this is my job. As in, my job right now is to probably go repair some ship. Which could take hours. Hours, that I do not want to spend in your company."

"How do you know it's a ship?"

"Because it's almost always a ship. We're here now though, so scoot." Holding up her ID card to the scanner, the door to hangar six slid open, just in time for a lab-coated scientist to come screaming out, his hair singed.

A terrible roar echoed through the hangar and Rosa and Kane gaped as a blonde woman in a purple dress breathed fire into the air. All around her, the technicians of hangar six were either hiding, running, or trying to do one of the two, their faces fear-stricken in the starlight from the large windows behind them and the firelight from the princess and the disaster zone she'd created.

Something in Rosa's gut twinged and a shiver went down her spine and all the way to the tip of her tail.

"I guess we found her."

Kane didn't respond, his mouth hanging open in awe. Rosa dragged him to the side of one of the few unharmed spaceships, pulling him out of the eyeline of the princess and nodding at the technicians huddled there too. One of the men rushed forward, grabbing Rosa by the arm.

"Rosa, thank goodness you're here. You can fix this right?" She recognized the man as Dr. O'fay, one of the head scientists in the outpost, but couldn't help but balk at him.

"Oh for- I am a mechanic. A mechanic. I don't specialize in fire-breathing princesses." Rosa glared at O'fay, but he just stared at her expectantly.

"Give me a break, Haverfield. You're the only one qualified for this kind of thing. Your work with the lupine was inspired! And that time with the seven hydraphines, too!"

Kane sent her a smug look and Rosa fought the urge to kick him. She should've just stayed in her pod this morning. She would have slept in, had a nice breakfast, relaxed-- but no, here she was. Twenty feet from a three-footed princess whose glass feet sparkled in the glow of amber flames.

"I'm sure all you have to do is talk to her and she'll leave us alone. At this rate, she'll blow a hole through the roof of the hangar."

Rosa glanced up, finding that the doctor was right. The ceiling of the hangar had begun to warp and bend due to the heat. The surrounding spaceships also suffered extreme damages. Rosa's knowledge of spaceship mechanics warned her that she really didn't have much time. Spaceship fuel, while not particularly combustible, was highly toxic. If the flame reached the fuel tank everyone in the room would die within seconds.

Which was debatably not a good thing.

"Doctor, I'm just as flammable as the rest of you." If not more so, but she knew he'd ignore that bit. They always did.

"Yes, but she'll listen to you. You're magnetic, these sorts are drawn to you." Rosa blinked at him, trying to understand how this man was a scientist. What an idiot.

"They are not drawn to me. That's not how it works. But fine, I'll talk to her. Then maybe I can actually do my real job."

Growling under her breath, Rosa clenched her fists, strutting out from behind the ship as calmly and confidently as she could.

"Elana? Want to cut that out?"

The princess's head snapped to look at her as her mouth closed, ruby lips shutting off the fire. Elana's blonde hair reflected the flickering light from the still smoldering flames of the ceiling and the burning spaceships.

"Who are you?" The princess's grasp of Aesaian, Rosa's language, was accented but clear. As was her hostility. Rosa smiled at her, the sick feeling in her stomach growing despite her mask of calm.

"I'm just here helping a friend. Now, want to tell me why you're doing this? You're pretty close to hurting someone." The princess tilted her head to the side, eyes squinting. Rosa straightened, her back tensing. She was being inspected.

"I think you understand well enough what I'm doing and why I'm doing it, silva."

Rosa's brow twitched. The princess knew what she was. Not that it was a big secret, but it made all the difference. She was the last of her kind in the galaxy.

"Do I?"

"You should. I doubt you want to be trapped here any more than I do. How do you like convincing poor unsuspecting beings to do what your keepers want? What do the old Earth tales call your type? Pied pipers?"

"That's really neither here nor there."

"Yes, and I'm sure you so like being their pet. That's what I'll be. That's what you are. Come on, silva, show a little backbone."Rosa crossed her arms over her chest, eyeing the shifting scientists and technicians still hiding behind ships and equipment.

"I have plenty of backbone, thank you. Now why do you think you'll be a pet? You're about to become the wife to the crown prince."

"Yes, like I said, a pet. I'll be what you call a trophy wife, perhaps literally. He did take my foot as a decorative bauble, after all. Tell me, do you think they'll do the same thing to your tail one day?"

Mind flashing back to the glass foot sitting on top of her desk and the blinking device coiled on her tail, Rosa contained a flinch. Elana gave her a knowing look.

"Oh I see, they practically already have. Well, that is the way of things."

"I'm not their pet, and you won't be either." The words tasted ashen in her mouth and one look at the expression on Elana's flawless face told Rosa that the princess knew it was a lie. Or at least mostly a lie.

Nothing ever was so simple for Rosa.

"I know who you are, Rosa Haverfield. Friend of the prince, outcasted when you thought too high of yourself and got your grandmother killed trying to make friends with a wolf."

The princess got it half-right, but really, that wasn't too bad. She got the important bits.

"Well I know who you are too."

Elana rolled her eyes.

"Who doesn't?" Elana took a step towards Elana. "But the real question here is what are you going to do?"

Rosa looked back at Kane and the doctor. Both of them watched, pure fascination on their faces, and dare she say it, greed. Kane looked at Elana like he might a rare species or a famous piece of art.

She hated that Elana was right. The red band on her tail glowed tauntingly and the nausea from before almost overtook her.

"Nothing?" Elana sounded disappointed. Swallowing, Rosa shook her head.

"No. I'm sorry, Elana." Taking a deep breath, she summoned all of her strength and tried to ignore the guilt. She could feel her vocal cords tingling, just waiting to be put to use. Her tail throbbed. Elana began to open her mouth, but Rosa beat her to it.

"Elana, keep your mouth closed and your arms at your sides. Do not move until I say so." The princess froze, and Rosa could see the anger in her eyes.

The princess had no choice but to listen. That's all she could do. Rosa felt Kane come up behind her.

"Good job, Rosa. I knew you'd come through. She'll make a great addition to the collection, don't you think? Never as great as you were though. You always have been the best."

"Thanks, Kane."

"Oh, and don't forget; it's your turn to pick this time. Who should be added next?" Kane stroked his blue beard, waiting for Rosa to answer.

Rosa closed her eyes. It was a good thing karma didn't exist. If it were real, she'd be dead by now.

She hated all of this. She hated that she couldn't stop. She hated that she was a coward. And she hated what she said next.

"I've heard about this princess with glowing hair..."

Beastly Beginnings

"Gael!"

Deep breath in. Slow exhale. Adjust grip on the blaster.

The museum's sirens blared as the monotone voice advised everyone to calmly evacuate the building. Nobody listened. A mass of panicked bodies flooded toward the exit gates, all with one goal. All except me, who tried to elbow my way back through.

"Jade!"

I open my eyes. The chaotic past fades away, replaced by the tense silence of the hovervan. The lights are off, but I can make out the outlines of other soldiers around me.

We all sit straight and unmoving. I can hear clothes rustle with every twitch.

The contrast tightens my chest. I burn for this to be the past. What would it be like if we had this level of calm in the museum? Oreven this level of alien awareness? Would I have been able to save them?

A crackle shatters the silence as my earpiece comes to life.

"We will be arriving in five minutes. Be prepared to disembark," Commander Royce says. "Inform me immediately if you require anything before then."

Everyone would have heard the same thing, but everyone remains stock-still. All we need is to prepare ourselves for the massacre that will come when we arrive at the Solvaro's lab. We don't know what they are researching, but our intel says its guarded and filled to the brim with alien scientists.

Maybe a biological weapon. Maybe a new type of bomb. Maybe a combination of the two.

"We're sorry, Gael. We found all of their bodies..."

My chest swells from an internal blaze as my vision flashes red. Five minutes can't come fast enough.

The minutes drag on as I mentally go through the different possible outcomes of the coming battle. I had just decided a bomb tactic that may cause multiple casualties when the hovervan began to slow. "Gael!"

Jade's cry echoes in my ear as the vehicle stops, fueling the fire within until it's a struggle not to charge ahead without everyone. Suicide wouldn't avenge Jade or my parents.

The back door slides open, and I rise along with everyone else. We file out in two lines. When I hop out of the van, I shiver. Our van and three others -- making sixty-four humans in total -- stopped in the middle of the woods.

I shiver. Once there would have been enough trees to make such a journey impossible. Jade loved going to the forest sanctuaries. They were so full of trees.

More trees -- another false promise the Solvaros never went through with.

"You okay?" a soldier from the line to the left asks. I think her name is Marlene, but I can't remember.

"Fine," I grunt as I reach up to touch the activation pad on my goggles. The eye set flashes, and then the dark night around me comes back into focus in black-and-white.

The soldier who spoke to me is still turned toward me, but after a moment, she shrugs and faces forward again.

"Everyone follow your respective commanders," Commander Royce says.

"Stay low. Stick to the trees. Don't drop your guard. And watch for the Solvaro's glow."

"Yes, sir!"

Our lines break apart, but each squad goes its own way. One squad to the right, one to the left, one around to the back, and then us, heading straight for the front. I know a fifth squad, the sniper unit, parked further away in search of higher ground.

The run is rhythmatic. Jog forward. Dart behind trees. Scan the area for any movement. Repeat. Our boots thud dully against the dry forest floor. A constant that seems to drag on but would shatter the moment the lab comes into view.

"Squad one, you are thirty yards away from the lab," the sniper commander says in my ear piece. Almost at the same time, a light breaks through the trees in front of us.

A smile spreads across my face as my pulse buzzes in my ears. So close. Mere minutes and we will be able to attack.

The trees thin as we get closer. The lab's top comes to view first, a rectangular tower with a dome top piercing the sky. A few moments later, the rest of the lab comes into view. It's a plain white building with lights flooding out of the windows.

My goggle's view shifts from the light. It changes from black and white to normal view, but a few spots stand out as a different color.

The red outlines of figures. Four that I can see, but I'm sure others wander around.

I duck behind a tree. Only five lines of trees and their shadows protect us from the Solvaro guards. Any closer and the guards will see us.

"The others will be in position soon," the sniper commander says. "Your signal to move will be our shot."

"Understood," Commander Royce whispers through the com. "Everyone, you heard Commander Kirigiri, be ready and hold your positions."

I shift my grip on my blaster and lean against the tree to steady myself. Just to wait now.

"Gael, are you sure you want to join us?"

"I've never been more certain of anything, Jax. I will murder all of them."

Commander Jax Royce's lip twitched as he sat back in his seat. "Well then, I suppose the Human Resistance may have a spot for you."

Four shots shatter the peace of night. It collides with one of the guards' shoulder and explodes in blue sparks against his armor. The guard cries out and grabs his arm. The nearest guard shouts to him in Solvarian while the others bring up their blasters and aim into the sky.

"Attack!"

We all move on Commander Royce's order. I twist around the tree at the same time as taking aim. The blaster hums with energy against my ear, crackling as I pull the trigger.

The others also fire. Energy blasts shoot through the air, flying in multiple directions. Some above, some to the left or right, and some straight in front of us. I curse. How many guards are there?

I've had many battles against the aliens, but never before did they end this easily. I figure at least twenty guards stood outside, but they didn't have cover, nor did they try to find any. Even if they got a few hits in, three minutes later, the Solvaro side lay lifeless on the ground.

"That was almost too easy," Commander Royce says from my right, confirming my thoughts. "You four" -- he points at me and three others -- "follow me. Everyone else, watch the surrounding area."

We form a wall around the commander, one on each side, and creep toward the guards.

Nobody shoots at us. Nobody charges from the doors or from around the building.

Once we reach the first guard, Commander Royce steps out from between us and crouches down by the Solvaro. He studies the body for a moment. The Solvaro guards have covered their entire bodies in armor reminiscent to a knights, but a dark grey rather than shining silver.

I prefer it this way. It blocks the Solvaros' unnerving body. Commander Royce seems displeased with it, though. He knocks his knuckles against the armor. My eyes widen.

The knock produces a hollow sound.

Commander Royce curses and yanks against the guard's head. As I feared, the helmet came off, leaving behind an open stub with wires sticking out.

Robots.

"Munroe, Grant, Zalaznik!" Commander Royce barks into his com. "Are you still engaged in combat?" He pauses. "Well, check to see if they're actual alien scum or if they're robots. Yes, I said robots!" Another pause, then he growls. "Heart of humanity, they were expecting us. And these dumb machines gave us away."

I frown. "How would they have known?" I ask. "The Galactic Union?"

"Must have been." Commander Royce stands again, glowering down at the robot."Someone must have told one of the human representatives. Traitors to their own race."

Anyone aligned with the Galactic Union betrayed their own race a long time ago, but right now we need to focus on eliminating the scum they aligned with. Commander Royce must be on the same line of thought because he turns to the door.

"Zalaznik, Grant, place your grenades along the front of the door, then come to our line." Commander Royce activates the squad com before continuing, "Be ready to charge."

I grin as we make our way to the forest line once more. "Explosive entrance?"

Commander Royce smiles as well.

"Explosive entrance. See if these pieces of space trash are as prepared as they think."

He then informs the other squad commanders of his plan.

Zalaznik and Grant place their grenades along the entrance and the surrounding wall, taking up fifteen or so feet. They jog over to join us when they finish.

"Is everyone in position?" Commander Royce asks the other squads. "On my mark, then, fire." He glances between Munroe and me. "When I give the call, shoot the grenades."

"Yes, sir!"

The night stills as we wait for the command.

I bring my blaster up and take aim at the grenades as I wait. Hurry up, I think. These Solvaro need to face their death sentence.

Commander Royce's com buzzes with activity, and he nods. "On the count of three then. One... Two... Three! Fire, fire, fire!"

We fire on command, hitting one grenade on each end. It doesn't take anymore. As one explodes, the one next to it does as well, demolishing the ground and wall around it in a brilliant blaze of fury.

Solvaros on the other side scream. They shout in their inhumane language, their fear flowing out of the building in waves. I soak it in as a save pulse of joy floods through me.

I have killed hundreds of Solvaro, but it hasn't satisfied the fire within yet. I'm not sure it ever will.

"Charge!" Commander Royce shouts!

We do just that, guns raised, ready to act as the avenging angels our world needed.

☆☆☆☆

Clack clack. "...mistake! We must..." Clack. "...no other way."

I groan as these words invade the thick blackness in my mind, punctuated by the occasional clack. It's annoying. Why can't I just sleep?

"So you are awakening, Gael Adams."

I don't recognize the deep, male voice that speaks to me. It has this strange throatiness to it that accents the word in a familiar way I cannot place.

Instead of replying -- which I'm not convinced I could do anyways -- I try to break out of the darkness still holding onto me. Something doesn't feel right. I feel weightless at the same time as weighed down. My eyelids refuse to open and my tongue fills my mouth in an unfamiliar way. The only similar experience I've had was when someone numbed my mouth to implant trackers. My mouth and tongue had tingled with numbness, yet their presence refused to leave.

"Gael Adams, can you hear me?" The voice again. It sounds distant. So, so distant.

What's going on? I push back against the darkness and struggle to reach into my memory. We charged the Solvaro lab. What happened after that? What happened?

My eyes fly open as it all comes back.

Rushing in, finding at least a hundred guards filling the central room, all of the Resistance pouring in just to find themselves outnumbered, the screams from both sides as blasts shot every which way, and then finally, our last ditch plan: bomb everything.

Only something went wrong. The explosion would be big, but there must have been something explosive because it seemed the entire world seemed to fall down in on us.

I shouldn't be alive, but here I am... somewhere. Wherever I am, there isn't much light. I barely make out large tubes lining the area in front of me. It takes my muddled mind a moment to realize I'm in one of those tubes. Blue-tinged liquid surrounds me. I reach up. Some metallic device is stuck to my mouth to let me breathe.

Had someone found us and put us into healing tubes? No, only the Galactic Union has such technology. Unless the Galactic Union is the one who found us...

"Well, you're awake, but I'm not sure you're able to answer me."

A jolt run throughs me, but my eyes can only drag themselves toward the one who spoke. My heart stutters when I see the speaker, then rams against my ribs as anger boils within.

A Solvaro stands in front of a computer, one hands still on the keys while he turns to face me. He wears a skin-tight outfit under a floor-length coat, covering most of his body, but his head remains visible. The sight sends my stomach into a squirming fit.

Solvaro are mostly humanoid aliens, though their heads are much more oval and smooth than ours. They lack hair of any kind, but that's because, unlike humans, they don't need it to keep them warm. They have another method, and that's what truly differentiates them from humans upon sight.

Their skin dances with light.

When the news first talked about the Solvaro, they compared their body to a lightbulb, something like our light panels but in a small bulb shape. Except the light they emitted didn't blind those staring at it. I can see the purple light within this Solvaro's skin, flowing like water.

The Solvaro stares at me, his glowing head tilted to the side. "Can you speak, Gael Adams?"

"Where am I?" I growl. The words feel unnatural leaving my mouth. My tongue is still too think and my jaw feels tight.

The Solvaro's eyes brighten as a small smile tugs at his thin lips. "Ah, very good! It seems the consciousness transfer is working." He looks back at the computer and taps a few things before continuing. "As for where we are, we're beneath the laboratory your team just destroyed."

"Where is my team? What have you done with them?" I try to push toward the glass, but the rest of my body is still waking up.

Again, I feel that sensation of being numb yet aware of my body.

The Solvaro winces and clasps his hands behind his back. "Well, you were the only one I found alive. I cannot tell you if any escaped though. Most of the surviving Solvaros left because they believed there to be more, so perhaps many made it to safety."

My heart constricts. So many human lives lost trying to destroy these monsters, and yet some live. I try to move again. Nothing. I need to get out of here and hunt down the survivors. Our loss cannot be in vain.

I squeeze my eyes shut as my neck tingles.

"What are you doing to me? Why can't I move?"

The Solvaro glances at his computer screen one more time before strolling over to me.

He scans me up and down before nodding in approval. "You humans have quite the interesting bedtime stories, you know that?"

He waits. When I say nothing, he sighs.

"Well, you see, Gael Adams, one of those stories I find interesting is something you call Beauty and the Beast."

I snort. "I ask you a question, and you start talking about some dumb kids story?"

His eyes do not waver. "Do you know the story?"

"All I care about knowing his how I can escape from here and rip your freak head from your shoulders," I spit.

If anything, my threat only amuses him.

"You see, Gael Adams, in the story, a cruel human is turned into a monster by a witch until he can find love with his beastly heart."

"And how does any of this answer my question?"

He considers for a moment, and then he steps away and gestures to the left. I slowly follow his gesture to find a human body laying on a table. I bristle. Did the scum capture one of our men? My mind is so caught up spinning with his intentions that it takes me a moment to take in the body.

When I do, the world stops, because cut up and burnt in a couple places or not, I can recognize my own body.

I jerk my head down. All I wear is pants, giving me a full view of my heaving torso.

Of my light-filled torso.

The liquid isn't tinged blue. It's turned blue reflecting the light coming from me.

The panic releases whatever had been stopping my movement. My neck stings as my hands fly to my head. Smooth, hairless skin. Oval shape. I lower my hands in front of me to see blue light moving beneath my skin.

"What have you done to me?" I shriek. I rub at my skin as if that will remove it, but it won't go away.

"I promise you all, I will kill every single one of them."

No, this cannot be real. They have me hooked up to a machine controlling my dreams. If I push hard enough, I'll wake up.

A machine somewhere beeps wildly as I continue to thrash and assault my skin. The Solvaro stands motionless and just watches my freak out. After a few moments, I give up trying to wipe the illusion away and snarl at him.

"Make this go away. Wake me up!"

"This isn't a dream, Gael Adams," he chuckles. "The contraption on your neck -- which I'm sure you've felt somehow by now -- connects your consciousness to the body of our poor, dead Solvaro friend."

"Then put me back!" I reach for my neck where I felt the sting before. Sure enough, there's a small chip the size of a coin. I dig my fingers around it.

"If you do that, you'll die, and I wouldn't recommend dying when you have a way back to your body."

I freeze, my eyes drilling into the Solvaro.

It may not be worth it to believe him, but I can't murder him if I'm dead. "And how do I return?"

"See, I explained that before, but you thought I was just gabbing out garbage," he says.

"Answer. Me."

"All you have to do, young Gael Adams, is feel love toward a Solvaro. Find love within that beastly heart of yours."

It starts as a chuckle, but then it grows into a full-blown, howling cackle. "Me?" I ask as a flaming tempest burns through my veins.

"Me love a Solvaro? You've lost your mind.

Now put me back in my own body!"

I pull my fist back. It's sluggish in the liquid around me, but when I throw it forward and into the glass, it shudders.

The Solvaro's eyes widen as he darts back to his computer. I slam my other fist into the glass next, then go back to hitting it with my other one. It's a pattern as the alien taps furiously into his computer, and each hit starts picking up speed.

A wicked smile spreads across my face as my latest punch leaves a crack. As I prepare the next hit, the Solvaro starts speaking.

"You have six months, Gael Adams. After that, your rose will have lost all of its petals, and the device on your neck will break. You will die."

Laughter bubbles out again as the crack spreads with my next hit. No, this isn't the end. I'm getting out of here and wringing that Solvaro scum's neck with the hands of one of his own.

I pull back both of my fists this time for one final strike. Before I can punch, a blast of cold, sweet air floods my air mask. My body instantly feels heavier.

No! I'm so close. I will my fists forward, but I know it won't work. They've lost too much power. No amount of willpower can help me shatter that glass now.

As darkness eats at my vision, my eyes drift over to my human body again. I know it's foolish and won't do anything, but I stop my attack to instead reach in its direction.

I don't want this. I want to be in my body.

I'm supposed to be avenging the family these monsters took from me, not becoming one of those monsters.

The darkness closes in, but before it can swallow me, I hear the Solvaro one last time.

"I'm sorry for the pain you must feel right now, Gael Adams, but I really do hope the Great Stars shine light upon your path."

Then I'm lost to the darkness. Just like that, my life as a human ends, and my damnation as a Solvaro begins.

The Three Bros Go To Mars

The first word out of his mouth is, "bro." It's as bad as I feared. Maybe even worse.

"Bro, this is it. We totally made it to Mars. Can't wait to start our vape shop. By the way, are you going to split that sub sandwich? It's way sloppy, but I think we can cut it in half," I hear the first colonist say as the trio of Earthlings departs the space ship perched on a red slab of Martian rock. They're three brothers, obviously. Just look at their matching noses; they're practically snouts. Or don't look, since I'm sticking my furry neck out from behind this boulder, watching the arrival of my new neighbors.

"Yeah, bro, it's going to be awesome AF here," the second colonist says, taking off his red baseball hat and wiping sweat from his brow.

He and his brothers are loud AF, too, even in the thin atmosphere of Mars. The air is still sparse despite how Earthling scientists a few years back engineered the oxygen mix with plants. It wouldn't be so bad, honestly, but the plants are these ugly, stout succulents. They installed them because they, "don't have to be watered." Except they do need water, eventually, which is why half of them are dead and the other half are dying. The plants, I mean. Not the people. Not yet.

"Bro, you smell that?" the third colonist says and sucks in air through his swine-like nostrils. "That's the smell of freedom to live the way we were always meant to: free porn, legal weed, and robots take care of all the boring shit like sweeping the floors and vacuuming. Welcome to the future, bro-skis."

"Yeah, bro, it's way different than Earth. Hashtag EEXIT," the first colonist squeals. "Hey, what about that sub sandwich? I'm hangry. Don't hog it all."

"Bro, I told you before. NASA didn't trust us with anything sharp on the flight over from Earth, so I don't have a knife. I can't cut the sandwich in half," the second colonist says.

"Bro, then how did there get to be so much mayo on that thing? You must've spread it with a knife, right? I mean, it's practically dripping off the bread, bro."

The second colonist raises his voice even more, "Bro, I got this made at Subway before we left. There's one here, too, somewhere, I think, probably."

"I thought you were watching your weight, bro."

"I am. Mayo is totally keto, bro."

The first colonist snaps his fingers. "Bro, I'm glad you're the smart one between the three of us, bro."

This conversation continues for the next 30 minutes. I listen to every word. I thought I passed out one time and was simply confused about the direction of their narrative, but, no, they literally restarted the entire conversation from the beginning, apparently forgetting that they'd already covered that ground about the sandwich and the knives. And then they high five. All three of them at once in a palm pyramid. Unironically. You can't make this up. I wish I was, because then I'd have a better reason for taking all this time describing this scene to you.

After the high five comes the complaining about the flight over to Mars from Earth. Chief among them: "the view is so boring," "the seats are cramped," "they overbooked the flight so I lost the seat I wanted in the emergency exit row," "security sucks," "the in-flight meals are too expensive," "I sweat like a pig," "they won't let you bring booze on the flight anymore," and "pretty sure they went through my luggage." All this despite the flight being free.

Mind you, they still haven't done anything yet. They stepped off the space ship and this is it. They're standing around arguing about the sandwich and complaining about the flight.

My notes, if they're correct, indicate they're supposed to be building a habitat for themselves. Martian dust storms can be awful, but they appear more concerned about the need to "check out the ratio on this tweet, bro" and to "see if my ex's Netflix password works on Mars, too," as well as the desire to "get a refund if Prime doesn't deliver in two days."

This throws off my plans. Expecting a team of skilled colonist-astronauts, I laid out building materials to lure them into a false sense of security. Three piles, to be exact, each selected for familiarity. The first is canvas and poles for a flimsy tent, ordered from Earth from a place called "IKEA." The second is plywood and nails, from "Home Depot." The third is called a "Starbucks" structure, which I assume is indestructible because of how frequently they appear on Earth. I'll destroy each structure one by one until the colonists are grouped together, then go in for the big kill. That's the plan.

But these three colonists are not astronauts. They're more like astro-nots.

Oh, no, their college humor is rubbing off on me, and it's only been 45 minutes. Time to take action before I start giving myself finger guns in the mirror in the mornings.

I reveal my position from behind the boulder. I point to the three piles of building materials. I shout, "Hey, I bet you could make some nice shelters with all this. Bro."

The three bros stop talking for once in their lives and stare at me. One of them says back, "I'm not your bro, bro. Don't bro me like that."

I'm a little confused at that response, so I say, "Aren't you worried about the dust storms?"

That same little shit says back to me, "Why don't you worry about yourself, cuck? You look like a mess with that long snout and four legs and big jaws and pointy ears and hair all over."

And then his "bro" chimes in with, "Yeah, watch your mouth, Martian, and show some respect for what we're going through. We're pilgrims, fleeing persecution from the snowflakes back on Earth, so you can take that attitude and fuck yourself with it."

It sounds unreal, but I'm telling you it's all true. They really say that. The cherry on top comes next.

"You know, bro, it's just like Martians to think they can tell other people how it is. They act like Earthlings are all planet-ists, but Martians are the real planet-ists because they get triggered by the stupidest shit and act like they're second to God because of it. They seem to forget that Earthlings built Mars themselves out of nothing with their bare hands. People like you and me, bro," the first colonist says.

"That's exactly right, bro," the third colonist says. "You can't even make jokes around Martians anymore. They take everything so seriously."

I groan and follow those gems up with, "So are you going to use your bare hands to build these shelters, too?"

"Fuck no. You're the Martian. Get off your lazy ass and come build these shelters," the second colonist says.

I can't make this up. I wouldn't want to make this up.

My patience is running very, very, very thin with these dolts, but I keep trying to get them to build the shelters anyway. I like it when things go according to plan.

"Dust storms. You must've heard about the dust storms, right? They're brutal. The winds will rip the skin off your face," I say.

"Actually, I'm skeptical about whether dust storms exist in the first place. How long have they been supposedly studying them anyway? A hundred years or so? That's barely enough time to come to a conclusion," the third colonist says.

"Skeptical," "supposedly, and "conclusion" are big words, so I ask him if he has a background in the sciences.

"Is someone paying you to ask those questions?" comes the response.

I give up.

On the one hand, he's right. Dust storms aren't due in this part of Mars for another week. On the other hand, even an idiot can be correct every now and then. On the third and fourth hands is nothing, because my two hind legs have fallen asleep with all this waiting around. I shake myself off to get the blood flowing again.

"OK, bros, tell you what. I'll leave you alone," I say and turn to leave. Looking back over my shoulder, I call out, "You're clearly the experts in this situation."

"That's better. We was kings on Earth. We don't need your handouts," the first colonist says and initiates yet another round of high fives.

They're not worth the energy. I go home to my cave one hill over, eat a couple Martian rodents, take a nap, and forget about my new Earthling neighbors. That carries through to the next day, and the one after that, and after that, until the dust storm finally hits. Then I remember. Listening from the protection of my cave, I swear I hear a scream for help. It could be that there really is one. It could also be my imagination. That wind will play tricks on your ears. It really will.

I shrug it off and go back to sleep. I'll check on the Earthlings when I get a free moment after the storm settles. Or not.

Bro.

The Hacker With The Glass Slippers

Alarms blare as Prince Richard strides into the security room. He tries to rub away the soreness from where his wrists had been bound, but the feeling won't go away.

"What's your report, Captain." His voice echoes through the white, cavernous room with the authority of his title.

Royal guards in their tidy red uniforms jump to attention. The room reeks of panic.

The crown prince joins the captain of the guard in front of video monitors that replay different angles of the unknown girl's flight from the palace. There's a smirk in her warm brown eyes as she looks back over her shoulder. She teases him. Catch me if you can.

"Your Highness," the captain says. His voice trembles. "We are having trouble finding her registration number. We've searched the invitations scanned for tonight's ball and one has been tampered with. It was just a shell. It didn't have a personal ID attached to it."

Richard folds his arms across his broad chest. "So we don't have a name. What about a ship? She can't have entered Sigyn palace airspace on an unregistered craft."

"The number was brand new, issued in the past week..." his voice fades.

"No name to that either?"

"No name." The captain continues his summary. "She left on an old planet jumper so she can't go far. Those things aren't meant for deep space."

"Assuming it hasn't been modified," Richard says.

"You really think her capable of that?"

"I wouldn't put anything past her." Richard smiles despite his wounded pride. "No, she hacked into our information archives. Alone. I need to know what she was looking for."

A woman with a tablet rushes up to them.

"Your Highness, the only files accessed in the last hour were the files on our proprietary terraforming technology."

Prince Richard's head snaps to look out the gaping window that faces north. Sigyn-9's atmospheric stabilizers glow on the horizon. A green light pulses against the night sky like the planet's heartbeat.

Genius.

The terraforming technology developed by the Sigyn Federation was the crown jewel of what would soon be Prince Richard's kingdom. That tech was worth more than any gem in their treasury. It was what made the Sigyn Star System so powerful — that they didn't have to rely on terrodomes to stay alive. An artificial magnetosphere meant they could do much more than just get by. Smart girl. The wealth of a kingdom at her fingertips and she chose knowledge. Dangerous girl.

"The files were downloaded to a storage device. They haven't been released onto an interplanetary computer network so that's a relief," the woman says.

The captain shakes his head in disbelief. "Impossible. She can't have downloaded them. Those files are too large."

"She put them in her shoe," Richard says.The two look at him, confused.

"She had on glass shoes. The heel of one fit into an access port and she downloaded the files onto her shoe. At first, I thought it might have been a key to get past the firewall of our archives, but it was her storage device."

"Glass shoes?" the captain asks.

"The right glass can store three thousand times more data than a computer chip—" Richard says.

"Sir." The female guard points to the looped video of a camera in the palace gardens.

"She dropped something."

The prince's heart stutters in his chest.

"Replay that."

The mystery woman's step stutters and she stops. She looks back at something that glints in the light of Sigyn's moon, Loki.

"Whatever it is, find it," the captain commands to a bunch of lower level guards.

* * *A lab tech takes a swab and runs it over the fingerprint-locked laser multitool and swirls the swab in a vial of clear solvent. She injects the solution into the mass spectrometer. The multitool is a piece of junk compared to what's available these days, but, it had special meaning to the mystery woman. In the time he'd spent bound and helpless on the floor of the archives while she hacked into the servers, he'd gained a few pieces of information on her.

"Since there's no salvageable DNA on this, the spectrometer will tell us where in this universe the thief came from," one of the lab techs says.

"All right then," the prince says. "Let's see if we can at least get a general region to start our search." He knew two things already. First, that the multitool had belonged to her father. Second, that she had been orphaned. These facts she'd offered when he'd mocked the outdated tech she used the unscrew the access panels to the servers. He wouldn't soon forget the glare she'd turned on him.The machine whirrs and after a while, beeps. A spiky graph appears on the monitor beside it. The tech slides her wheeled chair over to the screen. Richard moves to read over her shoulder.

"I'm impressed she made it through our firewall," the tech muses while she clicks through the data to see what the mass spec came up with.

"Really?"

"Yeah. I mean, hacking is hard enough, but our system's firewall is essentially impossible to hack. She's not just good. She's the best."

"The best?" Richard's lips lift into a bemused grin as he remembers the sheer bravado in her daring smirk at him.

The tech leans closer to her screen. "Ahhh... okay."

"What?"

"There's organic matter on this tool that originated in Nottinghamshire - a spit of planets outside the Alfheim nebula."

"Nottinghamshire.' Prince Richard's pulse races. "I can work with that. How many planets in the system?"

"Five, Your Highness," the tech says. "Only two are habited, though. There are terrodomes on Nottingham, but I can confidently say this tool has been on the surface of the other."

"And what's that?"

"A forest planet called Sherwood."Prince Richard smiles. "Sherwood. I'd better assemble a voyage then. I know someone who'll be wanting her multitool back."

* * *

CPSIA information can be obtained
at www.ICGtesting.com
Printed in the USA
LVHW052022090123
736787LV00009B/248

9 781837 617272